overload
edited by David Laurents

zipper books

Overload edited by David Laurents

Copyright © 2000 David Laurents
Zipper Books is an imprint of the Millivres Prowler Group,
3 Broadbent Close, London N6 5GG All rights reserved.

No part of this book may be reproduced, stored in retrieval system, or
transmitted in any form, by any means, including mechanicals, electronic,
photocopying, recording or otherwise, without prior written permission of
the publishers.

First printing February 2000. Printed in Finland.
Cover photography © 2000 Millivres Prowler

web-site: www.zipper.co.uk
• ISBN 1-873741-51-0

British Library Cataloguing in Publication Data.
A catalogue record for this book is available from the British Library.

Other books in the ZIPPER BOOK collection:

Forbidden Love
• ISBN 1-873741-37-5

War Stories
• ISBN 1-873741-38-3

Hard at Work
• ISBN 1-873741-39-1

Flashpoint
• ISBN 1-873741-36-7

Slave Academy
• ISBN 1-902644-20-4

Rough and Ready
• ISBN 1-873741-50-2

CONTENTS

The Vector Experiments Alex Corey	1
Practice Pony Lawrence Schimel	15
Lessons Jameson Currier	24
Snowbound Dominic Santi	36
Mind Over Matter Chris Leslie	45
In the Pitts Michael Lassell	60
Daddy Lover God Don Shewey	69
Full Service David Evans	84
Tantric Sex Dominic Santi	99

THE VECTOR EXPERIMENTS
by Alex Corey

In the dark, there's only one way to tell the twins apart: Tom's prick bends to the right, and Tim's veers left. For that reason, it's best to have Tom on my left and Tim on my right whenever they both have their cocks in my mouth. Otherwise, it would be a logistical impossibility.

When I'm positioned like that, my head trapped in their crotches, my hands running up and down their hairless torsos, it feels like I'm having sex in stereo. The twins move in unison; when one leans back, the other leans back, and when one caves forward into an pre-orgasmic groan, the other is sure to follow. I try to facilitate this by coordinating my own movements, by tweaking the left nipple on both their chests or dragging my finger from neck to navel at the same rate for each. When I switch to manual, I make sure to grab each shaft with equal pressure and to time my strokes precisely.

Perhaps my experience as a research assistant has rewarded me in this respect. After all, I first met these unusual young gentlemen in the name of science.

Tim and Tom appeared in cut-off shorts and tight white T-shirts one afternoon in response to an advertisement placed by my supervisor and graduate advisor, Dr. Emory Charles, a rather controversial psychiatrist who wanted to investigate claims of paranormal psychic activity between both identical and filial twins. He and I were overwhelmed by the turnout; thirty-four couples called in response to our ad, and we ended up accepting twenty-six for the study. For purposes of anonymity, we code-named them according to the alphabet; the first couple was Adams for A, the second Busby for B, and so on. When we got to Tim and Tom, the twenty-second pair to apply, we nicknamed them Vectors for V.

It was my job to perform the intake interviews, and while I now find it

The Vector Experiments

rather amusing that I regularly perform intake on *both* the Vector boys, our first encounter hardly suggested the eventual course of my own private experiments. I refer to my notes, transcribed from cassette as Tim and Tom started and finished one another's sentences (dashes indicate a change in the speaker, and though I neglected to note which of the two spoke first, I'm rather certain it was Tim for reasons which will soon become obvious):

"It's like I'll be lying there in bed at night and I'll just know he's out – you know, picking up some college girl, bringing her back to the apartment – and I'll know the exact instant he's got her between the sheets – and I'll know he knows – it just, like, happens – I'll be pumping away, just about ready to shoot off, and then bam! – there I am in my own bed creaming the sheets – and I'm thinking *my God, get the fuck out of my mind* – but he likes me in there, don't let him fool you – it's like having two orgasms, his and mine, only his are sometimes, well, kind of weird – he means, well, it happens the other way around, too – only I know he's not with some girl he's picked up – it's just different, almost more intense, like I'm – like he's doing it to me, you know? Like maybe that's why he's so into it – but in some ways, and I know this is gonna sound weird, it's like I'm doing it to myself – yeah, like he's fucking himself – kind of like an echo – and no matter when or where I am, I'm coming all over myself – it can be pretty inconvenient – like I was standing in line once with this chick at the movie theatre, and all of a sudden bingo! I'm filling up my briefs – or I'll be in a restaurant on a date, and I'm thinking *how am I gonna get over to the men's room without letting this guy see the wet spot* – and once I was in a locker room and suddenly all the guys are watching me get this amazing hard-on, and pow! I'm spewing all over the guy next to me – and believe me, when he spews, he spews! – but it's weird, you know, that we have this link to one another, because I'm straight and he's – heterosexually impaired, is what he's trying to say, but don't let him fool you, he can – yeah, alright, I've been known to swing both ways, but not all the time like you..."

And so on and so on. They went on like this for nearly half an hour, eyes locked on one another as they spoke, hardly noticing how I shifted in my chair and tried to rearrange the contents of my briefs so that my own arousal didn't interfere with theirs.

That arousal became shamelessly apparent with the next step, a brief physical exam administered by yours truly. The Vectors stood there side by side, T-shirts off and shorts unbuttoned, the waistbands of their Hilfigers slung low amidst thick patches of wheat-coloured pubic hair. I thought of how cute that was, how they had probably been dressing alike and acting alike since grade school. Now, in their late twenties, they probably still went on shopping trips together, just like they spotted for one another at the health club and visited the same hair stylist. They smiled at one another, daring and teasing, until finally Tim pushed his down and let his cock spring up to attention, a somewhat thin yet lengthy rod that, as I've noted, slanted perceptibly to his left.

When Tom pushed his jeans and jockeys down out of the way, his prick jumped up as well, though it took a moment to stiffen and stretch out the way his brother's did.

I recorded their specs: 6'1"; both about 185 pounds; hazel eyes; light brown hair; somewhat pale complexions; faint traces of body hair other than the underarms and pubic region; 40 inch chests tapering to size 32 waists.

This last measurement gave me a chance to witness their sexual rivalry firsthand. I had squatted in front of Tim with the measuring tape and was taking the reading when he used the opportunity to rub his cock against my arm. He made the movement seem involuntary, claiming that the tape measure around his belly made him ticklish, but when it happened a third and fourth time, I stepped back with a smile.

"Maybe I should just measure that cock of yours and to hell with the rest of the exam," I said.

"Never fails," said Tom. "No matter where he goes..."

"Aw, I'm sure he'll measure yours too if you ask him real nice," Tim said. He grabbed his prick and held it up toward me, gesturing at Tom to do the same.

So, for the record, there it was: both five inches thick at the base of the shaft, Tom a dark-veined seven and a half inches and Tim one of the sleekest eight inches I had ever seen.

Owing to the Vector twins' chaotic work schedule (Tim was a health club trainer; Tom a third shift press operator), Dr. Charles entrusted me with the

The Vector Experiments

initial experiments, which were to take place in the evening. Simply put, I was to verify or disprove the phenomenon of their simultaneous orgasms. To do this, I suggested that one of the twins be placed in a booth equipped with a two-way mirror, while the other sat in the lab with me. Video cameras would record the both of them, with the time measured in seconds at the bottom of the screen.

On the first night we met, Tom offered to go into the booth, claiming both birthright (he was technically fifteen minutes older than his sibling) and heterosexual privilege (which he invoked with a laugh). I went with him and wired him up to the monitors, affixing small sensors to chest, back, and stomach so that we might have a detailed record of his breathing and heart rate. I instructed him on how to affix a small metal sensor to the underside of his penis so that I might also keep track of blood flow. Brainwave patterns would come later, and then only if their claims proved true.

I left Tom in the booth with a couple of magazines – some back issues of *Playboy* that I had borrowed from the fertility clinic down the street and my own copies of *FreshMen* and *Torso* from home.

When I returned to Tim, he had stripped completely and sat spread-legged in a folding metal chair, his butt cheeks pressed against the green vinyl seat pad. The video camera stared at him from behind my own chair; a cart with another set of monitors stood to his left. I set about placing the heart rate and breathing sensors on his chest and stomach, noting that he flinched whenever my fingers pressed against his ribs. When it came time to attach the last of the devices, I made a bold move and grabbed the head of his cock, pulling the semi-flaccid thing out slightly so that I might tape the wire just behind the head.

Tim smiled. "Alone at last, and already you're taking advantage of me," he said.

"It's just part of the test," I said with a wink. "Another measurement."

I tapped the intercom button that linked our two rooms. "Any time you're ready, Tom," I said, then settled into my chair.

In front of me, the two small black and white television screens turned toward me showed both Vector twins – Tom leafing through a *Playboy* in the booth and Tim sitting patiently in front of me. When Tom found a photo spread he liked, he reached his hand between his legs and began to fondle his balls. In front of me, Tim closed his eyes and sighed. He grabbed the sides of the chair, perhaps remembering that I had forbidden him to touch himself. The muscles along his arms tensed as the rest of his body slouched forward, his hips pushing upward and out as though he were offering himself to me. His ass lifted off the chair slightly so that he looked like a gymnast caught mid-routine. Meanwhile, his cock thickened and stirred, then stretched out slightly along his left thigh.

Back in the booth, Tom had opened up to the centrefold and dangled the magazine in front of himself. His rod had stiffened considerably, and he stroked the shaft slowly, his fingers splayed in a delicate manner that seemed somewhat atypical of his personality. A minute later, his aggressive nature returned, and he grabbed at his muscle like it was the saddlehorn on a bucking bronco. His heart rate soared past one hundred, and his brother's followed suit.

In the chair across from me, Tim writhed in a nearly prone position. His toes curled under as he pushed his feet across the floor, and I watched as a tiny clear bubble of pre-cum pushed its way out of his prick-slit, smearing against his inner thigh as the head of his cock prodded the skin. I set my clipboard down on my lap and began to write, leaning down against the notepad to contain my own erection as Tim's lifted steadily upward.

On the video screen, Tom had thrown away the *Playboy* and now bounced up and down in his chair, his eyes pressed shut and his mouth wide open. I was tempted to turn up the volume so that I might hear his gasps and cries, but I knew that if Tim heard them, he might know when his brother were coming and ruin the test results.

Tim's erection was complete now, having completed a full 180 degree arc. The pale pink head of his upturned cock now bobbed just an inch or so away from his puckered navel and pointed up toward his smiling face. I noticed that his nipples had hardened considerably as well, tightening from their normal velvety flatness into nubbly circles the size of dimes. A slight sheen of sweat on his breastbone reflected the fluorescent lights above, and I recorded the wetness of the hair under his arms as well as the appearance of one sweat drop which coursed down along the inside of his arm.

The Vector Experiments

Pre-cum dribbled down each time Tim tensed his abs, leaving silver threads stretched between the head of his cock and his navel, in which a slick little pool had formed. The sight of so much liquid prompted a similar response in me, and before long, I could feel a slippery wet spot forming on the inside of my briefs. I shifted in my chair, but in doing so only allowed the head of my cock to push along my inner thigh and poke out of my underwear, leaving the head in direct contact with the blue scrub pants I was wearing.

Across from me, Tim's face contorted as though he were in pain. "What's happening?" I asked him. "What are you feeling right now?"

"Oh my God!" Tim's voice exploded. "I'm having an orgasm but I'm not coming. Or he's not coming. But I'm...I'm...right...there..."

On the monitor, Tom sped up his hand motions, jerking himself toward his self-promised moment of ecstasy. At last he shot off, huge spurts that he caught in his free hand. I quickly looked to Tim.

With his hands still tightly gripping the sides of the chair, the head of Tim's prick swelled and spewed a burst of jism against the underside of his chin. Bolt after bolt followed, the milky globlets spattering all along the length of his breastbone. Tim sucked his stomach in and gasped as the orgasm continued, sending shudders all through his body. The cum trickled in quick streams along the concave walls of his belly, puddling together with the pre-cum around his navel.

As the spasms subsided, Tim's breathing regulated, and as his chest and stomach filled once more with air, the jism spilled over and ran down his hips to drip onto the chair and the floor.

Tim stretched his fingers out and released the seat of the chair. His lips parted into a goofy kind of grin that one might expect in the cornfield but not the laboratory. He reached up and traced some of the cum-lines across his belly, sliding his fingertips back and forth.

Meanwhile, in the booth, Tom sat his with head between his legs, and whether he did so to keep from passing out or to lick the cum off his skin he never would say, but when I went in to remove the sensors, there were only a few splotches of semen on the floor, leaving a good palmful of jism unaccounted for.

We agreed to meet again three nights later so that the Vectors' roles might be reversed. They left with a cheerful glow on their faces, proud that they had passed my initial test with such flying colours. Tim joked that he wanted copies of the videotapes to send to all his friends at Christmas time, and I reminded them both of the confidential nature of the study. "Just joking, professor" he said, and he landed a soft playful jab to my chin as he stepped outside.

Once they were gone, I set the latches on the door and walked back into the lab, flicking off the switches on the various cameras and machines I had set up for our experiment. When I got to my station, however, I sat down and looked at the two small televisions, both screens now blank.

I rewound the tape of Tim to the beginning, then pressed play. As his smile flashed in black and white on the screen, I pushed down my scrub pants and reached for my cock. It was still half sticky/half slick with pre-cum from the experiment, so I had no trouble getting a quick hard-on. I timed myself perfectly, varying the speed and strength of my strokes so that at the exact moment Tim's naked body bucked and jolted in his lab chair, I added my own share of spunk to the floor around it.

Later, when I came back through with the mop, I took further pleasure in the fact that I was swirling his semen together with my own, and that some trace of that magical mixture was bound to remain behind.

Our second encounter began on a less productive note. Tim had been in the booth for fifteen minutes while Tom sat flaccid before me, his limp dick drooping sleepily across the green vinyl padding of the seat. On the camera, Tim flipped through the magazines, stopping here and there to read a passage in one of the short stories, at other times looking at the ads. When he got to a photo spread, he would look at each picture for ten seconds or so, then turn the page.

Finally he looked up at the camera and spoke. I turned up the volume. "What was that? I couldn't hear you."

"I said this just isn't working for me."

"Are you having an off night? Tense or nervous?" I asked.

"I'm just not used to magazines. I'd prefer more...I don't know. More

The Vector Experiments

action. More life."

"I can run home and get a video if you want…"

"That's not what I mean," Tim said. "And anyway, I think one of these electrodes is slipping off…"

I flicked off the intercom and looked at Tom. "I'll be right back," I said. I grabbed my clipboard and walked around the corner to the booth where Tim waited. When I opened the door, he smiled up at me.

"That's more like it," he said.

"What?" I asked.

"You."

Tim stood in front of me, his cock in his hand. "I need something more…interactive," he said. He reached for my hand and brought it up to his mouth, licking the fingertips before guiding them down to brush across his left nipple. He laid the flat of my palm against his stomach, then pushed down so that my index finger pressed into the swirled star of his navel. I poked at the nubby growth there, then stretched my thumb down toward the fine hairs of his crotch.

Tim guided my hand further down, releasing me only when my fingers had wrapped around his cock. The skin was stretched smooth and felt as shiny as it looked. My fingertips traced the contours of the shaft and head, circling round and round a slight cleft of skin on the underside of the tip.

Tim moved forward and kissed me, his lips as soft as pudding. Wisps of his hair tickled my forehead, and I could feel him blink against my cheek as his mouth moved lower, over my chin and along toward my neck, then onto my chest as his fingers pushed away the lab coat and quickly unbuttoned the shirt I was wearing. When he had pulled the shirt-tails up out of my pants and parted the flaps to expose my stomach, he sat back down in the chair.

"You've got a nice body," he said.

"I work out some," I replied.

"What's the rest look like?" he asked.

"It's fine," I said.

"Show me," he said.

Tim drooled a bit into his hand and resumed stroking his own shaft. As I pushed my pants down around my ankles, I reminded myself that I was acting in the name of science.

"I don't want to ruin your experiment," Tim said, "but I'm glad you can watch, and that I can watch you. You grab your cock, too."

I reached down and touched myself as instructed. My prick leapt to attention.

"Very nice," Tim said. "Have I told you about my little sexual sideshow?"

"No," I said.

"Check this out."

Tim stroked his cock slowly, then sped up, squeezing the flesh so that the pre-cum spilled forth from his slit. With one hand he worked his thickening rod, while the other stroked his torso, squeezing the nipples and fingering the navel, massaging the muscles that strained all over his body as he brought himself closer and closer to orgasm.

My own hand moved instinctively, working the foreskin back and forth along my shaft, matching the rhythm that Tim had set. Just looking at his torso, with the various coloured wires hooked up to the monitors, made me well aware of how much current and charge flowed through his muscles, all of that energy now focusing itself like so many rivers rushing toward the ocean.

Just as he was about to peak, Tim rearranged himself slightly in the chair and opened his eyes. "Show time!"

He smiled at me, then gave a series of short hard jerks on his cock. A white bullet of cum flung upward in a high arc; Tim opened his mouth and thrust his head forward, sticking his tongue out to catch the jism. I pulled harder at my own cock, overwhelmed by what I was witnessing. Tim's head bobbed back and forth as he caught the second and third shots of cum; for the fourth, he had to bend his neck slightly downward, and with the fifth the show was pretty much finished. The drops began to fall short, spattering on his chest and lower stomach instead.

Tim smiled, then swallowed. As I watched his prominent Adam's apple slide up and down, my own cock jolted in my hand, sending a first jet of cum on a short trajectory toward Tim and unloading the rest on my fingers as they swirled up and around the head of my prick.

"I caught seven one day," Tim said. "It's all in the wrist."

The Vector Experiments

He let go of his cock and jiggled his hand in the air as if to demonstrate, then laid his palm across his stomach and gathered up his juices for a finger-licking finale.

I watched intently, my own mouth watering as his hand went down for seconds and thirds, his fingers working around the electrodes, then squeezing out the last drops from his shrinking dick.

"I'm sorry," he said just before bringing that last bounty to his lips. "That was awfully rude of me not to share." He held out his hand, the index finger coated with creamy white.

"Maybe next time," I said. "I brought my own." I lifted my hand to show him, and he laughed as jism dripped like melting wax from my fingers. I watched a drop hit the clipboard at my feet, then remembered the video camera pointing into the room, and the fact that Tom had probably just shot his own load as well at the monitoring station.

I pulled up my pants, instructed Tim to do the same, and hustled out of the room, only to find that Tom had already towelled off, dressed himself, and headed outside for a cigarette.

At home the next night, I sat in my living room and watched the video of Tim once again. I had stripped down to my briefs, hoping for some relief from the heat and humidity that had persisted past sunset. In one hand I held the remote control for the VCR; with the other, I fondled my balls and cock. Once in a while, I'd reach out to a glass of ice water gathering sweat beads on the coffee table, dip my fingers in, and drizzle the cold water across my chest and belly before reaching back into my underwear to spread the coolness. The cotton fabric had become nearly see-through with wetness, half from the water and half from pre-cum.

As Tim began his triumphant spasms on the television, I pressed the freeze frame button and marvelled at his body, the beautiful grooves and plates of his abdominal muscles and the rounded contours of his shoulders and biceps. I pressed the slow motion button and watched frame by frame as the pearl of white streaked upward from the slit of his prick, a liquid blur except for its moment of apogee, the very instant that Tim's head darted forward and his luscious tongue reached out for the catch.

My cock pumped a hot load into my briefs, and a moment later, the phone rang in the other room. As I lay back spent on the sofa, I listened as the answering machine picked up, then smiled as I listened to Tim's voice on the line. "I just had the strangest sensation…"

The next morning, as I ate a breakfast of cold cereal and orange juice, I scribbled down some notes for our next encounter:

EXPERIMENT THREE
INTENTION: To determine the nature and effect of simultaneous orgasm in psychically connected twins when BOTH twins are engaged in sexual activity.

MATERIALS REQUIRED: Two healthy male specimens, born within one half hour of one another and possessing forceful libidos; one research assistant, ready and willing to administer whatever erotic pleasures are requested by the subjects.

PROCEDURE: Research assistant (RA) undresses the subjects and stands them side by side. RA fondles the genitals of both men until erection is achieved, then manipulates their penises to the point of orgasm, being careful to ensure that both men come at the exact same moment. RA than records the men's reflections on the experience.

At first Tom was hesitant, but the idea intrigued him. Oddly, the two had never thought to attempt a simultaneous orgasm, either by jacking one another off or by synchronising their sexual exploits. Tim responded to my suggested experiment with the glee of a child who had been told that Christmas was coming twice this year, and Tom soon relented under the condition that I clearly indicate his heterosexuality in my final report.

In the lab later that night, the two men stripped down, and we began.

For some reason, both men remained flaccid as I cupped their balls, even after my index fingers inched up toward their glory holes. When I turned my attention away from their cocks, I saw that Tom was watching me intently

The Vector Experiments

while Tim had closed his eyes.

"Maybe you should both close your eyes," I said to Tom. "That way it won't freak you out that I'm doing this."

"It's not freaking him out," Tim said. "He's just trying hard to make it look that way. Try harder, Tom. Harder!"

With that, Tom's prick swelled slightly and stiffened, as did Tim's. The sight of both cock heads lifting toward me triggered another idea, and I used my grip on their balls to pull them in closer. Their pricks stiffened even more as their legs and butts touched, and I watched with fascination as Tim's began tracking to the left, away from Tom's cock, which headed right.

"Switch places," I said, releasing my grip on them momentarily. They didn't ask why; they just did as they were told. I reached my hands up and ran my fingers along their torsos, comparing the prominence of ribs on both their chests, the slight outward slope of their stomachs toward the groin. Once more I cupped their balls, then lifted slightly to bring their cocks front and centre, the swelling pink heads just centimetres apart.

I pressed my lips against them, startled somewhat by the degree to which Tom's responded. Slightly bent as they were, the two cocks looked as though they wanted to wrap around one another in a fleshy braid. I pressed forward again, parting my lips to take them both into my mouth, an almost impossible fullness. My hands were free to wander around their hips, to stroke and squeeze the tight cheeks of Tom and the softer, more supple butt of Tim.

As my head moved slowly back and forth, I felt every part of them, from their knobby ankles to the sculpted indentation at the base of their throats, the highest point I could reach while sucking them off. Their smell was amazing, a heady blend of sweat that reminded me of the steam in a Chinese kitchen, the warm, damp presence of both sweet and sour. My appetite grew, and I took them deeper into my mouth, wedging my tongue in between their two shafts and then licking both heads on the pullback.

Tom shuddered, a tremor of abdominal muscle as I used my fingertips to brush past their nipples and ramble across the ridges of ribs. I raced across their bellies, then grabbed once again at their balls, pulling the sacs downward and away from the base of their cocks as I sucked them in. Tim stag-

...gered back a step, leaving me with only Tom in my mouth – Tom who suddenly went wild, his left hand reaching down into my hair and pulling me forward, turning what had been a rather textbook blow job into a total head fuck.

His cock took on immense proportions and stiffened well beyond anything I had observed in our earlier meetings. As I gave one last pull on his balls and moved my fingers further behind, I found out why; he had thrust two fingers up his asshole and was working them hard as he struggled to squeeze in a third.

Without warning, Tim reached around from behind me and worked at my belt, then unzipped my jeans and pushed up my shirt so that he could spread one hand briefly across my chest while the other dove into my briefs. His fingers fluttered around my prick like so many rose petals, their soft touch bringing on an erection so hard it hurt. Something flashed in the corner of my eye; I saw that Tim held a foil packet in front of me, the top ripped off. I repositioned myself into something less like a crouch and more like standing, even though I was still on my knees. Within a matter of moments, I could feel Tim's slender rod pressing up against my asshole.

Tim's was the smoothest entry I have ever experienced, and though our awkward position made for a slower ride than normal, it was the first time I can ever recall that I felt fucked with finesse. His cock became a vibrant part of me as it reached up inside, then slowly receded, only to push even further with the next careful thrust.

"I'm almost there," Tom said, and Tim doubled his efforts, making up for the moments he had lost earlier. I slowed my own motions, then took Tom out of my mouth and worked his rod with both hands.

"Almost...almost..." Tim said. He reached around me and grabbed at my cock again, timing his thrusts to match the hand job. I did the same with Tom, leaning back slightly so that I could get a better view of his massive tool and at the same time thrilled to feel Tim's stomach slapping against my lower back as he pumped upward into me.

We all exploded at once: Tim deep inside of me while his brother and I exchanged crossfire. All our bodies shivered in unison, every nerve sensitized from tip to root. For those few moments I lost all sense of identity and felt a multiplied rush, the splendour of six nipples tingling while numerous

The Vector Experiments

limbs entwined, the forceful pounding of three cocks blasting with enough firepower to bring down a fortress.

When it was all over, we toppled in on one another, laughing and panting, a pigpile of pleasure.

In my report, I recorded that we all saw hundreds of stars, but in different colours: bright green for Tim, yellow for Tom, a magnificent blue for me. Dr. Charles looked up at me when he finished reading the results in his office the next morning. "This, uh, experiment of yours seems highly unorthodox," he said, "despite the intriguing results. I'm not entirely sure I find it acceptable."

"I'm not sure either," I replied, a grin breaking out across my face. "That's why the twins and I have agreed to work at replicating the results."

"You mean do it again," Dr. Charles said.

"As many times as it takes," I said.

"I see," said Dr. Charles. "And have you given any consideration as to how this might influence your future here in the lab?"

"I have, sir," I replied.

"And?..."

"We've already taken an ad out in the local paper," I replied. "Only this time, we're looking for triplets."

PRACTICE PONY
by Lawrence Schimel

I couldn't help thinking about the sign I'd torn down from the post office door:

> PUT A BEAST BETWEEN YOUR LEGS!
>
> JOIN THE YALE POLO TEAM.
>
> INTRODUCTORY MEETING
> TONIGHT AT 9 P.M.
> IN THE DAVENPORT LOUNGE.

The yellow xeroxed sheet with this information was riding in my back pocket, folded into a tiny square, as I crossed campus. I couldn't help imagining myself astride a horse, the feel of withers pressing up against my asshole, rubbing back and forth... I was getting so hard I was sure that everyone walking past must notice my erection, and I swung my books loosely in front of my crotch, feeling like I was in high school again. Nostalgia 101.

I'd grown up on horseback, riding competitively in dressage and hunter-chases until I hit high school and decided it wasn't masculine enough. Even then, I knew I was gay, but I was afraid people would find out. In high school, it's just not accepted. So I did everything I could to pretend like I wasn't. In college, things were different, but I still wasn't comfortable being completely out. There were these football players who lived on my floor, who I had to share a bathroom with, and I was afraid of what they might do to me if they knew I was gay and thought I'd been watching them in the showers all this time, desiring them.

But the idea of polo was sexy – and very, very masculine. Despite the wording of their sign: Put a beast between your legs. Did they know what that

Practice Pony

sounded like? Could they mean... I was afraid to finish the thought, lest I jinx myself. I glanced at my watch, then thrust my hand into my pocket. Just eleven hours until I can find out, I told myself, hopefully, as I squeezed my hard cock in my jeans and walked into my anthro class.

I'd gone to the meeting for the Yale Equestrian Club during the first few weeks of my Freshman year, but when I walked into a room full of thirtysomeodd women I just pretended I had stumbled into the wrong meeting and fled. My heart had pounded in my chest as I hurried back to Old Campus and my dorm; no way was I going to be the only boy on an all-women team! That would've been like running through the streets shouting, "I'm a faggot! I'm a faggot!," and I wasn't ready for that. I'm still not, although I'm much farther out of the closet than I was last year.

I didn't think the Polo Team would be anything like the Equestrian Team. It didn't seem like a women's thing, so I was surprised to see four or five girls in the Davenport Lounge when I walked in a little before 9 p.m. But there were also a dozen guys sitting about, half of them in riding pants or chaps and boots. There was one man – and he was a young man, not a boy like most of the people in the room – seemed to dominate the whole room. His skin spoke of some exotic clime: Brazil or Argentina, someplace Latin, someplace where heat and passion were a way of life. He had liquid black eyes and lips that curled in a small pout when he stopped talking. Obviously tall, even though he was sitting on a couch, his long legs were casually spread wide...

I quickly looked away. Great first impression, Glenn, I berated myself, drooling all over the men.

But as I scanned the room and my eyes fell on him again, as he talked with a group of three very fresh-looking guys in jeans who stood facing him, I knew that I'd be joining the team if he was on it.

I struck up a conversation with someone I recognised from one of my Poli Sci classes, and after a moment Mr. Drop Dead Gorgeous stood up and called the room to order. He was even more attractive when standing, I thought, as my eyes travelled up and down his tall frame. The bulge in his crotch seemed even more enormous on his thin waist.

Turns out he wasn't just on the team, he was Captain. Which meant I'd suddenly developed a new hobby.

The smell of shavings always brings back the memory of the first time I'd sucked another man's cock: hot summer afternoon, one of the stablehands took me into one of the back stalls and dropped his pants. I'd been so enthralled by that huge, veined piece of flesh that swelled between his legs. It reeked of his sweat as I knelt down to examine it more closely; the whole barn reeked of strong scents: cedar from the shavings, the stale bite of the horse's urine, steaming mounds of manure baking in the heat. Pre-cum was leaking from the tip, and I reached out to wipe it away; my fingers burned as they brushed against the swollen, throbbing glans, but rather than pulling back I grabbed hold of his cock in my fist. It was easily twice as thick as my own, I marvelled, and half again as long. I'd hardly imagined cocks could be that size. "Suck on it," the stablehand commanded, pulling my head towards his crotch. There was no way I could take it, I thought, but as I opened my mouth to protest his cock pushed in and –

I shifted uncomfortably in my jeans, suddenly very aware of my surroundings in the Yale Armory. My cock was stiff as a polo mallet, and feeling far too confined in the jockey shorts I was wearing for a change. I'd want the support, I knew, once I was on horseback; I hadn't made allowances for getting such a raging hard-on. And staring at the Captain's tight ass in his riding chaps as we followed him to the arena wasn't helping it go away!

There were eleven of us left who'd been interested enough, after listening to the requirements for being on the team and the commitment we'd have to make if we joined, who were now about to try getting up on horseback. Many had never ridden before, so it was a chance for them to see what it was like, to get used to being astride a living creature. There were only four horses saddled up in the arena, so we took turns getting on and walking around. To keep us humble, if simply staying astride wasn't battle enough, we had to walk forward and try and hit a ball. It was hard enough just holding onto the mallet – I rode English, but you had to keep the reins bunched in one hand and neck rein like in Western styles, so that your right hand was free to hold the mallet. And when I tried to hit the ball! It looked so easy when the team

Practice Pony

did it, but I must've missed by four feet!

I kept guiding my horse around again, in tight circles, again and again, trying to hit that damned ball. But I never did. The mallet struck too high or too low or too far to one side. I was really impressing the Captain like this, I told myself each time, trying hard to fight the blush of shame and embarrassment that coloured my cheeks.

To my surprise, as I dismounted, the Captain said, "You've got a good seat and you ride well. But you can't hit the ball for shit. Meet me in the practice room at the gym tomorrow at 6:30."

My heart was beating so hard and loud I couldn't hear my own reply. I must've mumbled something. He hadn't offered anyone else a private lesson, so he must actually see something in me. My cock felt pinched in my jockeys again. I wanted to climb up into the hayloft and jerk off, but I didn't know how to get up there yet. I went into the bathroom, instead. My hand was covered with grime and horsehair but I didn't care; I fisted my stiff cock until I came, whispering "Alberto" as I shot my load against the white ceramic of the sink.

The gym was crowded with sports teams practicing after classes were done for the day, and also the many people who were simply there to work out or jog or swim. I wished I had an excuse to cruise through the locker rooms and get an eyeful of the sweaty jocks going into the showers, but I was fully dressed in my riding gear, even though I wasn't about to be on horseback, just the wooden practice horse. I'd thought it would make a better impression on the Captain, however, to show him I was seriously interested. Which I was–in him, more than in the sport!

I wandered down corridors, following the directions the guard downstairs had given me. Past the squash courts... there, on the end. A normal sized door with a small window at eye level. I peered in. It was empty, save for the large wooden horse in the centre of the floor. I tried the handle and the door swung in. The air was stale; the room hadn't been used in a while. Mallets lined one wall, and a few old balls that had lost their firmness.

I walked over to the horse, a simple wooden frame with stirrups on leather straps dangling from either side. I swung up onto it and just sat there for a moment, enjoying the feel of such a wide body between my legs. I put my hands on the wooden withers and rubbed back and forth, scratching my asshole through the fabric of my jeans and underwear. I imagined Alberto licking my ass, working my hole with his tongue to prepare the way for his cock...

I checked my watch, wondering where he was; I was still fifteen minutes early. In my excitement to see him, I'd made certain I wasn't late!

I ran my hand up the inside of my thigh, rubbing the side of my swollen cock which had poked free from the confines of my briefs. I wondered how soon he'd show up; did I have time to go jerk off? It would let me concentrate on the lesson at hand. But even if there was time, where could I do it? I looked over my shoulder at the tiny window in the door. Even though not many people came all the way down to the end of the corridor, it would be just my luck that someone would.

I dismounted and walked over to the wall to select a mallet. I would practice my swing, to take my mind off my aching cock. If I didn't lose this erection by the time Alberto showed up there'd be no way he couldn't notice it. I chose the longest mallet and climbed back on the wooden horse. I stood up in the stirrups like they'd shown us yesterday and took swing at an imaginary ball. The mallet cracked against the side of the horse and I winced at the sound. I was glad no one was here to have heard that, and also that I wasn't on a real horse! I took another swing and this time managed to avoid hitting the horse, although I still couldn't keep the mallet directed where I wanted it.

Again and again I swung, trying to get accustomed to the heavy weight at the tip of that long stick, its arc as it travelled towards the imaginary ball.

"Your mallet is too long."

I was on the follow through of a swing and I almost swung myself right over the side of the horse I was so startled by his voice.

I turned around. My heart was beating so fast from fear, and staring at him it felt as if it wanted to stop; he was so hot! He was a tall shadow in the dusty light; dark hair, dark skin, and those liquid dark eyes...

So much for having forgotten my erection, I thought, as I twisted back to resume my proper seat and break eye contact.

"I hadn't realised you were there."

He walked toward me; I could feel his presence behind me, just beside

Practice Pony

the horse. He exuded an energy, something sensual that sent an electrical charge through my body. My swollen cock thumped against my leg each time he spoke, vibrating to the timbre of his voice.

"I told you six thirty. That was ten minutes ago."

My eyes flicked to meet his; he'd been watching me for ten minutes! I couldn't read anything from his expression, so I looked away, down at my hands in my lap, the reins bunched between them and the mallet jutting off to one side like a giant erection. I let the tip of the mallet dip; it helped to hide my real erection.

Alberto took hold of the mallet and handed me another one.

"This is a better size for you."

The new stick was half a foot shorter. I leaned over the side of the horse to try and touch the floor, and almost slid off I had to stretch so far.

Alberto laughed, a short quiet burst of sound. "Much better." I turned to look at him, and he met my stare. I couldn't read him at all, which is part of what I found so sexy about him; he was a cipher.

"You've got to stand up in your seat when you swing."

He offered no more explanation, so I went ahead and tried it, assuming that's what he wanted me to do. I stood up and leaned forward to take a swing, and it was much easier to keep the head of the mallet focused where I wanted it to go. I wasn't entirely convinced it was the size of the mallet, however, except the fact that the shorter mallet was, as a consequence, lighter. I'd just spent a good twenty minutes swinging that first mallet, so I felt some of my skill had simply been my own practice.

I took another swing with the new mallet, and then another. Alberto didn't say anything, just watched me from beneath those dark, brooding eyes. I kept practicing. Occasionally he would comment, in the form of an instruction. "Slow down the swing." "Lift your arm higher."

"Take off your jeans."

I looked at him, surprised. Had I heard him correctly? My heart was beating so fast I could almost hear it rev; I could hear nothing else. At last, this was the moment I'd been hoping for! Then, why was I hesitating?

I dismounted and looked up at him. He hadn't moved. He was watching me, casually, almost disinterestedly, waiting. But he was watching me.

I stripped down for him, peeling off my chaps slowly, giving him a bit of a show. I undid the buttons of my jeans and remembered suddenly that I'd shaved off all my pubic hair the other week. What would he think? I worried, as I stripped off my underwear with my pants. As I bent over to step out of each leg my erection was pointing straight at him, so hard it was throbbing like a discotheque. I couldn't believe what I was doing; this was a public gym! What if someone walked past and looked in? But right then, I couldn't care about anything but Alberto and what he wanted from me.

Naked from the waist down, I climbed back atop of the practice horse and stood up in the stirrups, my ass up in the air as it had been when he asked me to take off my pants. My sphincter twitched, anticipating the feel of him sliding into me. I thought of him using his crop as a dildo, thrusting the long black leather whip into me... A bead of pre-cum dripped onto the saddle.

Pain flashed across my buttcheeks!

I spun around, almost falling to the floor before I realised where I was and caught my balance in the stirrups. I sat down and gripped with my knees to keep my seat in the saddle. My ass burned against the leather, a strip of heat-pain.

He'd whipped me!

"I didn't tell you to take your chaps off," he said.

I dismounted again. He was standing much nearer to me this time, I could feel the closeness of his body, making my own respond so strongly. He saw all of me, naked before him, so obviously desiring him, but he made no move toward me. I had to wonder what he planned to do with me, or to me. Whatever it was, my body wanted it, and was ready for him.

I bent down to pick up my chaps and couldn't help looking at his basket, which always bulged so prominently I couldn't even tell if he was hard now or not. I climbed back into my leathers, pulling them over my legs. My ass and cock were left bare, and it felt as if a sudden draft snuck through the tiny window, deliciously cold and making me even harder.

I climbed back onto the practice horse and resumed my position in the stirrups, leaning forward over the neck, my ass thrust into the air.

He tapped the inside of my leg with the crop and I tried not to flinch. Slowly, he tapped his way up my inner thigh, sending goosebumps across my

Practice Pony

skin.

He tapped my balls, on either side, making them swing.

He didn't say anything about the stubble.

Suddenly the crop was gone. I wanted to turn around and see what he was doing, but I stayed where I was. I strained to hear what he was doing, listening for a rustle of fabric, a footstep, anything, but there was no sound of any sort – I couldn't even hear if he were in the room with me.

There was a rush of movement behind me, and I sat down to turn about – I sat right onto his cock. I cried out, unprepared for this impaling; heat flared through my gut. I hadn't even heard him move, not to unzip his pants, or unroll the condom he was wearing, nothing. His cock was long and thin, like his body; it seemed I could feel it inside me, well above my navel.

"Grip with your knees."

I did so, pulling myself up off his cock a few inches. I held there a moment, and then he stood up in the stirrups to slide into me once more, pushing me forward with a grunt. I leaned into the wooded neck again, wrapped myself around it and held on for dear life.

He laced his fingers through my hair and jerked my head back, so his hot mouth could more easily find mine and forced it open. My jaw ached as his long tongue snaked its way down my throat. He reached under my shirt and seized a nipple between his thumb and forefinger.

I arched my back with the sudden pain. Alberto thrust into me, grinding forward. My cock slapped painfully against the polished wood. I reached down and grabbed the reins; I looped the leather cords over my balls so every forward thrust made them tug my cock.

His breath was hot in my ear, pulsing rapidly in horse-like bursts from his nostrils. I couldn't hold back; I'd been so excited thinking about him for so long, I shot my load onto the horse's neck, letting it ooze down the length of the wood. He didn't stop thrusting into me, riding my ass relentlessly, thrusting into me deeper and deeper. My insides felt like they were being torn apart. But he didn't stop, and soon my cock grew hard again with his filling me up.

At last, he too came, crying out in a short bark as his body spasmed, then silence. His long cock was still within me, upholding me and holding me up.

He dismounted, and I slid down against the wooden horse. My ass burned; it twitched against the smooth polished wood. I collapsed against the wooden neck, my cock slicked by my own cum as it slid between my stomach and the wood.

"You've got a good seat," he said. "But you've still got to practice your swing."

LESSONS
by Jameson Currier

There was a time in my life when I became a virgin again. It was during a period when a lot of things were going wrong, or, rather, a lot of people were disappearing from me without saying goodbye, and those who weren't disappearing were afraid that they would be disappearing soon themselves, too, and so, instead of waiting to see if I was going to vanish as well, I sequestered myself instead. I drew those willowy pink chenille curtains of mine closed, locked those overpainted louvered window gates up tighter than a chastity belt and decided to hide in the dark away from it all until it was safe to go back out in the sunlight again. It never really got safe again, you know. Things never really got better but I learned how to adjust to them; I learned to peek through the slats and wear sunglasses and hats and whatever other protective gear I could get my body into when I went outside. But then one day I found myself no longer fretting about my self-imposed exile and back out in the sun again – in Sheep Meadow in Central Park carelessly sunbathing with my shirt off without even putting sunblock on my skin, no less – and falling in love with a married man who was trying to fall out of love with his wife.

It was a complicated relationship for us both right from the start. Even though those gates of mine had been closed so long that even the locks were rusty, I was nonetheless definitely standing outside my closet door. He, alas, was hidden within his. But none of this hampered any of what happened between us in bed, of course. In fact, that's where the relationship, well, blossomed and grew, to mix a few metaphors. Soon enough we began experimenting and, well, his greatest desire was for me to teach him how to become a bottom, or, in more technical terms, how to become "the passive partner who receives the penetration of a male's penis." And I became more than a willing coach for him, never one to shy away from the kind of muscular, beefcake ass he possessed. I spent hours getting that sphincter of his to relax, lubing up a small butt plug until he was comfortable with holding it inside his ass, then progressing to inserting a slender dildo, then gradually moving up to a larger one, then a wider one, until one day we reached the point when he was ready to take my cock up his ass. I remember thinking at the time, that if someone had bequeathed me that sort of time and attention then I would have no desire to want to find another boyfriend. I'd want to get married.

I should have realised during all these lessons that Trilbys don't stick around to marry their Svengalis. Once my boyfriend had mastered my cock, he soon began requesting to play the new role of top to my bottom. The only problem was, he wasn't interested in giving me the time and attention I had given him, nor was he interested in giving up being a bottom, either. Like I said, it was a complicated relationship – I was out and he was in and he wanted to be in and out with other guys. I never had the chance to switch from top to bottom with him, because we were too quickly switching between other partners and fighting too much about our positions. But he wasn't the only guy I had dated who, well, wanted to flip me over, if you catch my drift.

I should probably admit now that to many men I seem like the ideal bottom – boyish-looking and short, I don't even weigh in at 150 pounds. Which is why, I think, I get such a delicious personal pleasure out of so often turning the tables and demanding that I be a top with all of those, well, you know, hunky macho guys who want me to roll over and play bottom for them. But the truth is, even though I looked boyish and my boyfriend wasn't really my boyfriend anymore, I wasn't really boyish any longer. I suppose this is a round about way of saying that I wasn't getting any younger. And, as community folklore has it, of course, after so much time goes by, those closed gates soon look like a boarded up wall; if you want to open the window, you have to start over again and knock out a hole if you want to see the sun. And so here I was a virgin again after all these years of isolation and waiting for the right guy to knock my window open.

The real truth is: I was a single and unattached aging gay man yearning for love. What I wanted was to find a better man than the kind of man I was

Lessons

usually meeting, and one of the methods I thought that might help me in my personal quest might be if I were to, well, uh, make myself more versatile in the bedroom department. Knock my own gate down before someone else hit a brick wall, if you know what I mean.

And so, not long after that insight, I began perusing the personals in order to meet my dream man, a habit I had gravitated to for years and years and years whenever I felt the dating pool was rather shallow. I picked up newspapers and magazines at the bars, the community centre, the bookstore, the newsstand — wherever I could find one which carried men-for-men personals. At home I would sit at my desk with a red felt-tip pen poised in my hand, ready to circle the most desirable ones. No matter how many personals I circled and notated in the "Romance Only" or "Let's Date" sections, I always seemed to ponder more and more over the "Raunch and Kink" or "Sex Only" sections, fascinated by the obsessive nature of so many gay men and at the same time frustrated that so many guys were looking for such specific requirements in order to obtain pleasure, and knowing, really, that my nature would most likely preclude any visits to the kinkier sides of gay life. The only thing I had ever desired out of a perfect sexual encounter was to give as much pleasure to my partner as I wanted him to provide to me. And that didn't necessarily include smelly jock straps or foot worship, though it also didn't preclude them either. And so one particularly lonely and forlorn day this ad caught my eye:

B U T T PLAY 101
Let me teach you how to enjoy your ass and
asshole. I will show you how to experience
ultimate pleasure from the space between
your legs.

I must confess now that I had never answered a sexual ad before. Yes, I read them and mulled them over, but I only circled and called the romantic, dream date ones. And as for sex, I'd always found enough action at the bars or the clubs or on the street or from the dating ads that I hadn't ever needed to turn to the "Sex Only" personals as an outlet. My goal was to find a worthwhile long-term relationship or at least someone who would stick around after the third date, not someone who wanted to stick their sticky fingers up my butt in order to get their rocks off. Nonetheless, I circled the ad, part nostalgic over my lost boyfriend and part curious about whether I should really consider a new method to snare a new one. A few days later when I was leaving voice mail messages for all of my potential dream dates I decided, oh, well, what the hell, let's respond to the butt player as well.

None of my Perfect Husbands responded, but the butt player did. Our short, introductory conversation on the phone went something like this.

"So you're into butt play?" he asked.

"Not really," I replied.

"You ever had anything up your ass before?" he asked.

"Not in a while."

"I've helped a lot of beginners," he said.

"I'm not exactly a beginner," I stated, "just starting over."

"Boyfriend?" he asked.

"Not any more."

"I can see you Sunday at nine," he said. His voice was cheerless and perfunctory, making it sound as if I had called for a doctor's appointment for a shot of penicillin. But it was exactly this sexless, clinical exchange that made me so easily accept his offer.

"Okay," I answered. We talked a few minutes more. He told me his address and that his name was Joey. He admitted that he was in his early fifties and had gray and black salt-and-pepper hair. As I hung up the phone, I reminded myself that this was a learning experience – he was going to teach me to be a bottom, or, well, teach me to be a better bottom. Henry Higgins wasn't exactly the perfect man for Eliza Doolittle when they met, either, you know.

I arrived at Joey's apartment nervous and tipsy and more than fifteen minutes late, which (even on gay median time) is more than a rude way to begin an association. I had indulged in a glass of wine at the bar on the corner of Joey's street, a trendy little smoke-filled, artsy-fartsy place with skinny women in black dresses and guys in dark T-shirts and gold hoop earrings. As I gulped

Lessons

down the last third of my drink, I had reminded myself once again that this wasn't a date. This guy didn't advertise in the "Looking for Love" section, and I wasn't expecting Joey to be my Mr. Goodbar. He was only Mr. Chips, after all, and I could leave him as soon as he taught me, uh, well, how to enjoy the pleasure of a man's penetration.

"Want something to drink?" he asked me when he ushered me inside his apartment. My distress must have clearly shown on my face at that moment. Joey was more like sixty than fifty, and his salt-and-pepper hair was an unshaven beard. Otherwise, he was bald as a cue ball and had a puffy face that looked like a sandbag that had been punched and not regained its shape back. He was slightly shorter than I was but more than three hundred pounds overweight, a fact which he hadn't mentioned to me on the phone. He was dressed in the kind of light, blowzy outfit that when worn by street people make you immediately cross to the other side of the street. If he had not lived in one of those high-tech, luxury, contemporary apartments that always seemed to end up photographed in Metropolitan Home or the Thursday section of the Times, I would have turned around and left, because this potential deamboat more closely resembled my worst nightmare.

I should probably add that the Sunday night I arrived at Joey's apartment, it was a warm, misty late spring evening that seemed to possess more humidity and mugginess than actual heat or raindrops. I stood in his doorway with a moist umbrella and my split ends growing into an afro. I felt so, well, old and troll-like myself at that moment that I was conscious I was standing on a clean beige carpet, worried that I had brought with me all the urban dirt and soot and grime I had carefully tried to avoid out on the street. Joey's apartment was clearly more showplace than a home. The smell of a bouquet of flowers which rested inside a crystal vase on a table near where I stood wafted up to my nose as I shook myself out of my damp jacket. The vestibule where I stood frozen like a stray dog that had been rescued opened up into a living room which was entirely decorated in beige – a sofa and matching wing chairs were upholstered in a neutral, beige fabric; prints of blank beige-coloured squares framed by beige wood were hung on a beige-painted wall; a shiny beige lamp rested on a shiny beige end table.

"Any wine?" I asked Joey as he led me to the sofa. I took a cautious seat, resting my derriere lightly on the edge of a cushion as if I were going to leap out of the room at any instant, because I was embarrassed at shedding particles of dust into the immaculate surroundings. Beside me, a beige coffee table jutted out close to my knees, empty except for several Playbills arranged in the shape of a fan.

"Red or white?" he asked.

"Whatever's open," I answered.

During our entire greeting and exchange, Joey was beaming as if a Christmas gift had just walked through the door. I sat waiting for him to return, feeling like I had played this game a million times and was too old and tired to try it again tonight with an ancient schlumper.

"I loved this show," I said, trying to deflect my discomfort when Joey returned with a glass of wine that looked more beige than white. I reached over and plucked a Playbill out of the arrangement, the fan quickly disintegrating into an unorganised mess. As I tried to straighten it all up the thought occurred to me as I made an even larger mess that murderers don't like show tunes – do they? But wasn't Joey too old to be a murderer? Isn't it usually the wealthy sixty year-old man whose throat is slashed the next morning? Joey seemed unperturbed by the mess I had made on his coffee table. In fact, he seemed to be a bit too amused by my nervous stumbling about, as if I were a six-month old child who had tottered into the room on his own two legs for the first time and he was about to applaud at any minute. When I looked up I noticed Joey was smiling, or, rather, I noticed that Joey's mouth had widened to reveal a set of conspicuously fake beige teeth.

"The dancing was terrific," he said, "but the music was abysmal." He waved his hand in the air on his last word, as if shooing away a fly, but then he started talking again about a theatrical wig maker he knew who worked backstage and, as the gossip started flying out of his mouth, his hand took to waving back and forth as if were a flag flapping in the wind on Independence Day.

I didn't really mind all the talk about the theatre, however. I was grateful for the distraction from the matter at hand. We sat and kibitzed about a lighting designer stepping out of his boundaries to become a director and a composer known for his S&M tendencies. In fact, we talked so long about the the-

Lessons

atre, that I completely forgot the reason why I was there in the first place. Joey was becoming a friend, not a potential teacher, and his fuzzy potato head no longer looked as if it belonged to a derelict. I could see the honesty in his face even if I couldn't imagine him successfully pleasuring my ass. But then Joey abruptly ended the conversation by leaning over and saying, "Well, shall we get started?" Suddenly his wrist was no longer limp but firmly placed against my shoulder and reaching around to remove my empty glass from the coffee table.

"Uh, sure," I answered, not really certain I wanted to go through with it.

"You can leave you clothes on the chair," he said to me as a doctor might say before leaving a patient alone in a room. In fact, Joey did leave me alone in the room when he left with the empty glasses in his hand, but he had returned by the time I had managed to stand up from the couch and fumbled with the buttons on my shirt. Joey walked to set of louvered doors which I had thought was a closet, but after he had opened them revealed a full-size bed built into a small nook that must have once been a laundry room. Along the bottom of the bed were a row of drawers built into the frame and Joey began pulling out an assortment of materials from the middle drawer: a pair of latex gloves, a box of condoms, a giant industrial-sized bottle of lubricant, four or five different sized dildos, none of which I felt certain that I could accommodate, a box of baby wipes and a plastic mat, which he unfolded and placed on top of the beige bedspread. I was deliberately wasting my time with my clothes, folding them and refolding them as he moved swiftly about his little alcove. Finally, he turned and looked at me standing sheepishly in my underwear and T-shirt.

"I sterilise all the dildos in the dishwasher," he said, as if that was the most crucial concern I could find about sticking a giant object up my ass.

"The dishwasher?" I responded, flabbergasted by a mental image of a row of dildos sitting straight up in a car wash. The next thing I knew I was standing behind him staring at the paraphernalia on the bed, all articles which had been withdrawn from the drawer in order to entertain my ass. Things had never seemed this complicated when I had played the same game with my ex-boyfriend. But that was the difference, wasn't it, I reminded myself. It was a game with my boyfriend. This was a lesson.

"And I always use condoms on the dildos," he said. Next, he patted the plastic mat on the bed. "Take your shorts off and sit up here," he added. Joey seemed to realise as he said that that there was no place for me to sit on the bed because of all his equipment, and he started rearranging things to make a space for me, or, worse, make a place for us. I realised the moment that I dropped my briefs that I should have thought twice before agreeing to all of this. Was I that desperate to learn how to enjoy my ass? Shouldn't I have really concentrated on finding a boyfriend first? I looked down at my cock and noticed it was smaller and more frightened than I had seen it look in years.

"Have you had many responses to your ad?" I asked, when I was seated on the edge of the bed, shifting myself onto the mat. Somehow Joey was already completely undressed and I was amazed that his body looked no different than when he had been wearing his billowy outfit. His body was as lumpy and wavy as beige fabric that had been sat on all day. The only difference between his body and his clothing was a chain around his neck that dangled a gold Hebrew symbol, now visible against the sparse, gray fluff of his chest. And then there was his erection, too, of course: a small, slender dick which popped straight out at me like a breadstick misplaced in an Easter basket.

"Nope," he said. "You're my first. I just took the ad last week."

Great, I thought. I'm a virgin again. And a guinea pig. And stupid.

But it was then that the lesson began. Or the life unfolded. Isn't that what teaching is all about? The passing of knowledge of wisdom gained not so much on one subject but on the cumulative experiences of many.

"When I first met my lover I was strictly a top," Joey said. I was on my back with my legs bent and my kneecaps parallel to the ceiling. "I wasn't interested in somebody sticking something inside me, because all I wanted to do was to stick something myself, you know. Then, after we were together for about four years, we started changing roles. He didn't always want to be the bottom so I experimented with it some and decided I liked it so we changed roles. He was the top and I was the bottom. That lasted for a few more years and then he decided he wanted to be the bottom again. That's when we started getting all this stuff," he said, waving his hand at his assortment of dildos.

"I think that's more than I can handle," I said, twisting my body to look at

Lessons

the smallest dildo, which in my estimation was about twelve inches long and eight inches wide.

"You think so? We'll see."

Joey had positioned himself at the end of the bed, a plump round period to my wavy exclamation point. He lifted one of my legs and rested it against his shoulder. The next thing I knew, his wet gloved finger was in my rectum and I could feel him twiddling with my prostate gland. I leaned up to watch his hand inside me, expecting him to say at any point, "Scalpel," or "Sutures," but instead he said, "You're very tight."

I nodded, wishing that there were some music playing or somebody kissing me or a video being shown or, better yet, that I had another glass of beige wine in my hand. Instead, all I heard was Joey beginning to breath harder, like someone who has asthma. I lay back down against the mat, hearing it crinkle as my skin pressed against it. I closed my eyes and tried to imagine myself a thousand miles away, but, instead, only heard the "slumpf, slumpf, slumpf," of Joey pumping more lubricant out of bottle and into his hand and then into my ass.

"It's the small ones that are the hardest, you know," he said.

I leaned my head up again and looked at him in surprise. "It's the truth. It's all about stretching. The walls don't stretch that much with the tiny ones. The big ones just force you to relax in order to accommodate them. Give me a big, fat dick any day. It's so much easier to manage and it's a lot more fun." He started laughing, a high-sounding hiccup that started in the back of his throat and ended with the quivering of his shoulders and saggy chest.

It was such an odd moment from someone I had heretofore regarded as a clinical, professional worker. "It's all about relaxing, you know," he said, still chuckling. "Once you learn how to relax those muscles down there you can take a football. I had a friend who used to work in the emergency room, and he used to tell me about all sorts of guys coming in with cucumbers or tennis balls or light bulbs stuck up their asses."

The thought of a light bulb up my ass was definitely unappealing, and I pumped a swipe of lube from the bottle and wrapped the oily palm of my hand around my cock, trying to force myself to become harder. Above me, I heard Joey gasp.

"What's wrong?" I asked.

"Ahh, why did you do that?" he asked.

"Do what?" I asked, shocked.

"I wanted to suck your dick. Now I can't take it in my mouth. And you have such a beautiful dick."

"Ohhh," I said, sorry, really sorry, that he hadn't acted quicker. "Thank you," I added, feeling like the moronic pupil who had disappointed the teacher.

Next, he took a slender dildo which I hadn't noticed before, the kind I had once used on my ex-boyfriend, lubed it up, and inserted it into my ass. It went in easily, though I could feel the walls of my ass caving into the dildo instead of stretching them further. "You've been practicing," he said.

"Not really. Those Kagle exercises don't work for me."

"Oh sure they do," he said. "You're just uptight. What are you so nervous about?"

Life, I thought. I'm nervous because I'm still alive after all these years. The only thing that worked out for me was that I didn't die when everyone else did.

"Open your eyes," he said and lightly slapped my chest.

I could feel the residue of lube where his hand had grazed my skin.

"I'm not going to hurt you," he said. "I won't do anything you don't want me to do. You can trust me. In a few lessons, you'll be able to take King Dong over there."

"King Dong?"

"The super deluxe double headed one," he said and nodded at the giant dildo with a cock head on each end. "My boyfriend and I used to play with that one a lot. There was a time when we were both bottoms. Come to think of it, there was a time when everyone in the city was a bottom. It sure was difficult to find a top some nights."

I gave him a smile and leaned back and started pumping my cock again. I felt myself growing thicker and he took the slender dildo out of my ass and lubed up a wider and longer one. Before I knew it, it was inside my ass, and I was rock hard, pumping my cock and arching my back away from the mat. And then I suddenly felt a decade younger, and a memory washed over me

Lessons

of a man I had dated on Fire Island. Joey bent my legs and rubbed my thighs just as the man had. And then he kept the dildo far up inside me, cupped my balls and rubbed them with his slippery hands. Then he reached one arm up and twisted my left nipple.

"The first time I was fucked, my boyfriend was so impatient that he made me bleed," Joey said. "I turned him into a great lover, though. Then he left me. Then he came back. Said he couldn't find anyone better in bed. Oh, he could find others to have sex with, don't get me wrong. But none of them had my touch. It worked for both of us though. He made me feel so beautiful."

Joey was breathing hard through his mouth by now, and he moaned and moved one hand to my cock and stroked it as he returned to lightly pushing the dildo in and out of my ass. "That okay?" he asked.

I nodded back at him.

"I miss him," Joey said. "He died about three years ago."

He stopped pushing the dildo in and out of me and pulled himself up out of his hunched over position. "That doesn't bother you, does it? Everything we're doing is safe."

I nodded back at him again that it was all right to continue. I was aware that we hadn't kissed one another, aware that not a single drop of body fluid had been exchanged between us. No tears. No sweat. As I looked at Joey's face as he worked over my ass and cock, alternating one hand between stroking his cock and my own, I realised he had survived, as I had, but his road might have been more difficult than my own. I sensed that the puffiness that bloated his face was not entirely the results of the ravages of aging but from the use of medication or the overuse of alcohol.

But I also realised he was enjoying his task, the first time it had occurred to me that he must have taken the ad out because he enjoyed sticking something up a guy's butt, enjoyed giving a guy pleasure this way, that perhaps maybe this was his fantasy, his fetish, the scene he wanted to play. Older teacher instructing the younger pupil. The thought of it made me smile and the delight surged through me light a jolt of electricity. I felt my body finally become sensitive to his touch. My first shot came like a wave of release, replaced almost immediately by a flood of tension and pressure and then a second shot into Joey's waiting palm.

Before he had a chance to remove the dildo from my ass or wipe my cum from his hand, I reached my hand up and clutched his cock and gave him a few quick pumps with my slick, hollowed fist. He came instantly, his come spurting over my wrist and onto the mat with a plop, plop, plop. He laughed as he caught his breath. "Thank you," he said.

Thank you, I repeated in my mind, embarrassed that he had thanked me for letting him fuck me with a dildo and then quickly jerk him off. As I dried myself off with the baby wipes and paper towels, it occurred to me then that teaching was such a selfless act. In that way it bore such a striking resemblance to being in love, doing something for someone else without the expectation or need of anything being returned. You don't expect someone to thank you. Lovers can be the best teachers. And teachers can be the best lovers, too. But I was aware that my encounter with Joey had not been without a certain level of self-absorption and self-need. His. And mine. Joey had knocked a window out in my wall for me. And I think I had helped him withdraw some quirkiness from his drawer.

When I was dressed and standing at the doorway in my still damp jacket, Joey held his hand out for me to shake. Instead of taking it, I leaned over and kissed him on his fuzzy cheek. He smiled and held the door open for me. As I stepped outside, I realised that I had revealed so little of myself other than the intimacy of my body. I hadn't even told him about my ex-boyfriend. But it was already too late. I felt myself headed back into my shuttered, private little world. But before he closed the door behind me, I turned back and said, "Thank you. It was fun."

And then I was back out on the street again, slapping my tennis shoes against the puddles of water like a teenager, eager to be a teacher again.

SNOWBOUND
by Dominic Santi

I should have worn long underwear. While the insanities of the New Year's "Y2-Khaos" stories were still getting plenty of attention, blizzard warnings had been at the top of the local news all afternoon. The sky was already dark grey, the temperature was dropping rapidly, and the wind was getting nasty. But I was tired, so I didn't stop to add the extra layer of thermals under my flannel and jeans for my weekend trip home. Instead, I threw my toolbox in the trunk, hopped in the car and hit the road. Even though I hate it when my balls get cold, I figured I'd beat the storm if I left work a half hour early.

I really wanted to get home. No hot dates or anything. I was just sick of the long-distance commutes that construction electricians like me get stuck with in the winter in Wisconsin. I was also grouchy from dealing with the tons of unexpected computer-generated glitches with which my company had rung in the new year. I wanted to spend the evening on my own couch with my feet propped up in front of the fireplace, maybe wrap up in a blanket and beat off while I watched the hot new "All Male XXX" video I'd picked up. And I wanted a good beer – a nice thick stout – none of this cheap industrial swill that seemed to be all they carried at the place our crew had been staying lately.

I'd gone too far to turn back when I realised my mistake. The wind was stronger than I'd expected. When the first snowflakes started falling, visibility went from bad to nothing real fast. By the time the highway patrol closed the interstate, my shoulders were stiff from fighting the gusts, and I was shaky from where I'd almost lost control on a patch of black ice.

The cops herded us all onto the nearest off ramp, towards a cluster of chain hotels and fast food joints that looked way too much like the ones I'd just left. The parking lot I pulled into was almost full. Grumbling to myself, I took my best guess at where the lines would have been and parked next to a red Toyota that was already half buried in snow.

The wind blasted into me as soon as I opened the car door. The icy air went right through my jeans. I could almost hear my nuts start chattering. And by now, I was getting hungry. Cursing myself for being too dumb to go south for the winter when even the damn ducks did, I zipped my parka and I headed in to see what rooms were still available.

There wasn't much. According to the computer, I got the last nonsmoking room – a double. As soon as the clerk handed me the key, I went into the restaurant to get something to eat. The wind was howling so loudly the window panes were shaking, and I was chilled to the bone. I figured dinner would warm me up as well as fill me up.

The food wasn't gourmet, but I didn't care. At least it was hot. Their beer though – damn, why can't these places carry anything good? "Yes, sir, we've got both kinds of beer – Crap and Crap Light." What I wouldn't have given for a Guinness right about then.

I was polishing off my chili cheese fries, still muttering to myself, when I felt somebody looking at me. You know, one of those little twitches that makes you look up to see who's there. Not that it took much to distract me. Aside from a few quickie features on the latest Y2K disasters, all the tube had was a continuous "live action" report on the storm. Yeah, I knew it was snowing.

The desk clerk was standing in the doorway, pointing towards me. My hand froze on the way to my mouth. The guy next to her was gorgeous. I mean, he looked like a movie star. Dark, wavy hair pulled back in a ponytail, thick mustache, shoulders out to here. I could see the muscles tapering down to his waist even through the flannel shirt. His open collar showed he'd been smart enough to wear thermals. I sighed, half in lust, half in envy. No doubt even the sizeable bulge in his jeans was nice and toasty.

Mister Movie Star smiled as he approached my table.

"Max?" he asked, sticking his hand out to me. "I'm Gerry. Mind if join you?"

His grip was firm and warm, like the smooth baritone rumble of his voice. He had one of those friendly smiles that made me feel like I'd known him forever. But I was too stunned by his looks to do more than mumble hello to him.

Snowbound

My hand tingled from where it had touched his. I could feel the heat down south as I responded to the sparkle in his deep brown eyes.

Fortunately, Gerry didn't have any reservations about carrying the conversation. "The clerk gave me your name – asked me to talk to you. Seems the hotel is about out of rooms, and they're getting a lot of families in here now. She was wondering if we could double up since your room has an extra bed. They'll waive the extra person charge, and I'll split the room cost with you."

He smiled again, but this time I saw the beginnings of shadows under his eyes. In spite of the twinkle, he looked as tired as I felt.

"I know it's an imposition, but I'm beat. And I don't want to sleep on the floor in here with a bunch of screaming kids."

As he spoke, I realised there were a lot of kids running around, even in the bar. The noise level had risen enough to drown out the TV. Not that I was cared – there was still nothing on but the weather updates, and those weren't changing. Then I noticed the manager dragging rollaways into one of the conference rooms attached to the restaurant.

I knew I wouldn't mind spending the night with Gerry. I just didn't know where his interests lay. I wasn't getting any kind of a vibe from him – other than tired. Then I decided it didn't matter. Just looking at him was warming me up in all the places that mattered.

"Sure," I shrugged, wincing as I drank the last of my beer. "I just hope their beds are better than their beer."

Then Gerry said the magic words. "I've got a couple bottles of stout I picked up at a microbrewery. They'll freeze if I leave them in the car. Want to help me with them?" He laughed out loud at the look on my face, slapping my shoulder as the waitress came up to take his dinner order. "I'll take that as a yes."

I was still trying to figure him out as he wolfed down a burger – no onions, extra ketchup. But by the time he was done eating, it was too noisy to talk much. There were people everywhere. I gave him the room number, and we went to get the stuff from our cars.

It took me a few minutes. Everything in my part of the parking lot was completely buried in snow. Fortunately, somebody had been to the red Toyota recently – one of the doors had been opened – so I found my car without too much trouble. I pulled out my overnight bag, and at the last second I grabbed the two emergency blankets I keep in the car. By then, I was freezing again, and I hurried up to the room.

Gerry was waiting outside the door. As I walked up, he grinned and held out the two bottles of stout. I didn't recognise the label, but I'll try most anything once.

I was still smiling at the thought of a thick, creamy brew as I opened the door and we walked in, stomping the snow off our boots. Then I flicked on the light and we both stopped in mid-stride. There, in the middle of the room, in all its solitary glory, was a lone double bed.

"Shit."

I don't know which one of us said it. We just stood there with the wind and the snow blowing in around us until finally Gerry pushed the door shut. I could not believe it. Trapped in a hotel room with a gorgeous and probably straight man – and one bed. Just looking at him made me horny as hell, and now there was no chance of a subtle seduction, much less of having any beer when he left.

Apparently I didn't hide my reaction quickly enough.

"Hey, don't worry about it," Gerry said as he walked across the room and set the beer on the table. "Computers are fucking up all over. I'll go back down and settle with the clerk. It's your room, after all. You can even keep the beer."

As he spoke, he kept his eyes on me. I felt the heat tingle in my icy crotch. So I figured I'd go for the blunt approach, while I still had the chance. I tossed my stuff on the floor and leaned back against the wall.

"It's like this," I said. "You're still welcome to stay here. But I think you're attractive as all hell." His eyebrows lifted, but I kept on, shaking my head to keep him from interrupting. "Don't worry. I'm not going to make a move on you. Well, unless you want me to. But I can't promise what I'll do in my sleep, and I don't want to get punched out for having horny dreams. So take your pick – a cot in the restaurant, the floor here with the blankets," I motioned towards the ones I'd brought in from the car. "Or the bed and me." I looked over at the table and sighed. "And it's your beer. You can do what you want with it."

Snowbound

I stood by the light switch, so he'd have plenty of room to go around me if he wanted to leave.

Gerry's smile caught me by surprise. He walked over, dropped his bag, and braced his hands on either side of my head. Then he kissed me – a long, slow, wet liplock that left me speechless. When we came up for air, he pulled back just far enough for me to feel his breath over my lips.

"I'll take the bed and you, Max. And I brought the beer to share." Then he stepped back, locked the door, and started stripping off his snow-covered clothes.

For a second, I stood there like some sort of ice statue. Then I came to my senses and peeled off my outer layer of clothes as fast as I could. The snow was melting in the heat of the room, though it was still way too chilly for comfort, and I really shivering from the cold damp of my jeans. The tail of my flannel must have pulled out when I was rummaging in the trunk, and that was soaked too. But I had dry socks in my carry bag. So I hung my wet clothes next to Gerry's in the shower. Then, wrapped up in just my socks and briefs and a blanket, I sat down at the table with my dream date to drink my beer and watch the latest update on the weather.

The report hadn't changed, but the beer was good. And Gerry looked mighty fine wearing just his wool socks and his thermals. I swished the beer around in my mouth, savouring the rich creamy taste. It was an imperial stout – cold as the room temperature, with a nice alcohol buzz.

Gerry was obviously enjoying his beer, too. He leaned back in his chair, scratching his balls from time to time as we talked about the usual stuff – where we were from, our favourite breweries, our jobs. He's a carpenter, which explained the shoulders. About the time I was halfway through the bottle, I started thinking about seeing just how much heat was emanating from that basket he was playing with, though it seemed only polite to wait until my hands had warmed up before I did anything.

I didn't get a chance to make the first move. As I was taking my last swallow, Gerry walked over and ran his hands up my blanket-clad arms. The next thing I knew, he'd leaned over me and we were kissing again. This time I could taste the soft fuzz of the beer in his mouth as he stroked his tongue over mine. His hands were inside my blankets, pinching my nipples into hard little points that felt tighter than frigid air could ever make them. Each time his fingers twisted, a flush of heat rushed to my crotch. Pretty soon, my cock was pressing hard against my Jockeys and I was trying to ignore the fact that my covers had fallen open.

Damn, but that man could kiss! He sucked my tongue and licked the insides of my lips. He even stopped playing with my tits long enough to pry my mouth open and trace the outline of my teeth with his fingertips. One minute his tongue was in my ear, the next his lips were moving down my neck and over my collarbone, sucking and tasting and generally making me pant like a dog. Then his fingers tugged on my nipples again. I was getting pleasantly sore, but his kisses were so hot it wasn't long before I was leaning into his hands and moaning as the blanket slid off my shoulders.

"You like that, Max?" he laughed. When I nodded, he leaned over and licked the point he had trapped between his fingertips. Man did I jump! So he did it again, blowing on the wet skin while I shivered. I could smell the beer on his breath each time he laughed.

Then he started on the other side. My head was thrown back as he knelt next to me, sucking on my right tit. I reached down for the bulge in his long johns. His basket was as heavy as it had looked. I admit it, sometimes I can be real impressed by size. And his balls were way more than a handful. I imagined they were cloaked in warm silky fur that would feel like a ski scarf against my face. Okay, so I was getting a little carried away. But the room was still frigid, and I could tell he was a bear by the way his skin crinkled under the heavy knit. I love warm, hairy balls. I gave his my full attention.

And his dick was leaking. Not too much, the cloth around the thick tube was damp but not soaked. In spite of my fascination with his balls, I definitely didn't want that treasure to get chilled. Gerry groaned when I touched him. I tugged him to his feet and leaned forward, rubbing my cheek against him. His cock strained towards me as it got harder. All I could think about was how velvety soft his bare skin was going to feel. I wrapped my lips around the long, thick bulge and blew, smiling as the heat of my breath leaked back out of the fabric against my lips. Gerry grabbed a fistful of my hair and yanked me to him, hard, while I nuzzled him some more.

It wasn't long before he was panting. Gerry pulled me to my feet and we dove into bed, still wearing our underwear. I'd dropped my chic designer caftan while I was playing with him. Now I was shivering and swearing against the icy sheets.

"You're freezing," Gerry said, sounding surprised. I'd curled up into a ball trying to condense my body heat. He rolled me over and pulled me into his arms.

"I hate this fucking weather," I muttered through my chattering teeth. "I could really do without this 11 months of winter shit."

His chest rumbled as he laughed and rubbed his hands over my arms and back. Then he stopped.

"Jesus, Max, you really are cold."

He sounded worried. I tried to laugh it off, but my voice came out sounding weird with my teeth knocking together. The covers lurched around as Gerry peeled off his thermals. Then he pulled me back into his arms, and I melted into him. The man was a fucking furnace! I snuggled up against the thick pelt that covered his chest, I suddenly wondering what felt better, those warm furry walls of muscle, or the thick hot cock pressing firmly against my belly. He tugged at the waistband of my briefs, so I kicked them off somewhere under the covers. I gasped as our hard cocks touched and he started kissing me again.

I'd never met anybody who could kiss like Gerry. Even my toes felt warmer as he probed and licked and sucked, his soft wet lips and tongue exploring each corner of my mouth, tasting my neck and face. And his balls were every bit as hairy as I'd dreamed. I shivered again and he hugged me to him.

"You ever seen those coffee heaters, Max? The ones where you put the probe in the coffee to heat it up?"

"Yeah," I said, confused. I was distracted by the feel of his tongue and the hard velvet heat of his cock rubbing against mine. Then the fog lifted. Oh, shit. I felt him smile against my lips as I stiffened. He knew that I'd figured it out.

"Roll over, Max. I'm going to I warm you up."

For a second, all I could do was groan into his kisses. Then I felt his hands on my shoulders as he pushed me over onto my side.

It was freezing outside of the covers, but I didn't have to get up. My carry bag was on the nightstand. I poked my arm out and dug in the side pocket until I found some rubbers and the lube. Damn, that lube was cold! A minute later, Gerry slid into me, and suddenly I knew just how that coffee felt. I could feel myself getting warm all the way through. When he reached around and wrapped my cock in his hand, I shivered all the way up my spine.

He stroked a couple of times, in me and over me. I just lay there gasping. I mean, I love getting fucked. To me, nothing in the world feels better than coming when I've got some guy's hard dick stuffed up my ass. Even the burn in my asshole felt good as Gerry inched his way into me, pressing forward until his wonderful, furry balls were snugged up tight against my asscheeks.

Then he was pounding into me, and I couldn't do anything but lie there with my leg lifted and rock against him. His hand moved over me in rhythm with his thrusts while his long, thick dick massaged heat deep into my joyspot. I shivered at the warmth of his bare chest and strong arms rubbing against me, and at the friction of his cock drilling into my ass. Even my balls were warm, and I wasn't shivering with cold.

It didn't take me long at all. It was one of those slow, sleepy comes. Gerry was in me so deep, pressing against my prostate so hard, the juice bubbled up out of my cock. I shook like my bones were breaking, gasping for air as Gerry's hard, warm hand pulled the come from my balls. I felt his heat all the way through the latex. Then his whole body stiffened and he shoved up hard against my asscheeks, his cock stretching me even wider as he gasped and surged into me. I shuddered again, this time with him, groaning as his climax pressed the last juice through my cock. My butt purred happily as Gerry relaxed against me with a long, contented sigh.

I turned to kiss him, and he lifted his head to meet mine.

"You warm now, Max?" His lips moved against me as he smiled.

I nodded, kissing him again before lay back on the pillow. Yeah, I was warm all right.

When Gerry pulled out, I grabbed some tissues and tossed the rubber at the trash. Then I snuggled back down into his arms. From the feel of the air on my nose I could tell it was still colder than hell outside of those covers. But Gerry was spooned up along my back, and we slept like a couple of bears

Snowbound

hibernating in a den.

The next day the news said it had been one of the windiest, noisiest blizzards on record. I wouldn't know. I couldn't even tell you if Gerry snored. I slept like a fucking rock. But man, was I warm.

Turns out Gerry and I only live an hour away from each other, and he brews his own beer. To my way of thinking, there's a lot of potential here. I'll find out when I visit him next weekend. I'm bringing some Guinness with me, and I'm not wearing my thermals. Starting the year 2000 with a late spring sounds just fine to me.

MIND OVER MATTER
by Chris Leslie

I'm walking home from work, on the last leg of my trip from my office job in New York City. I come to a corner and check out a guy waiting at a bus stop, he's really cute and makes my dick come to life. He doesn't pay me much mind but I look back anyway, if only to get a better look at his face. He sees me look out of the corner of his eye and spits into the street, but not in my direction. I smile as I feel my dick swell in the loose folds of my jeans. I put a hand in my pocket and squeeze it hard, sending a familiar rush through my body.

It's been raining, but now there are just a few lost drops of water in the air. I work the graveyard shift, starting work at midnight and getting off at eight in the morning, and walking home against the tide of commuting wage-slaves never fails to entertain. The weaker majority in their trench coats and ponchos shiver and hunch their shoulders in the cold aftermath of the storm. The swarthy figures in their slickers are still going strong. A glimpse here and a rub there, coming home from work is one long dick tease.

It's been one year and seven months that I've broke up with my boyfriend of five years, it's been eight months since I gave up on the idea that independent publishing would take in enough money to support me and took an office job to pay the rent. It's been three years and two months that I've fallen through the cracks of New York City's sidewalks, joining the men who walk about the city stroking their dicks, riding the ebb and flow of a sexual high. It's been a year and four months that I've been taking notes on these adventures and transforming them into *Dirty*, a magazine I publish independently. It's been a year since I got my first gushing fan letter, and eleven months since I got my first letter from a freak wanting sex.

Freedom and servitude. I read the graffiti on the storefronts and telephone

Mind Over Matter

poles on the way home, thinking what would have happened if I had followed this one, had spoken to that one. I reach the building where I live and someone has cut up my front door with yellow spray paint. I can't quite make out the words, but at least it's a sign of life. I never see anyone tagging, and wonder at the new scribbles that appear each morning, seemingly soaking through the paint like phantoms. Without fail, my landlord will be on the stoop this afternoon, painting over the new graffiti in a battle against an invisible enemy.

Once inside my bedroom I pull the heavy shades over my windows and drop into bed, half dressed in yesterday's underwear and a T-shirt I've been wearing most of the week. As always, getting into bed makes my dick spring to attention, and I start to pull on it a little, meditating more than masturbating, and I think of the boy at the bus stop, who I see nearly every morning now, and the guy who I met at the All-Male XXX last weekend who wanted to fuck me but hasn't called, and as I drift off to sleep I'm wondering what my life will be like when I'm thirty.

The ringing telephone wakes me around seven o'clock. While I don't often give out my phone number, I can't place the caller's voice and he won't tell me his name. I am not foolish enough to try and guess – such games can be disastrous. Finally, he says that he was glad that he had run into me and was sorry that he had lost my number.

"Aw, so kid it's you." I don't remember his name.

"In da flesh," he says with a hip-hop flourish. "So what you doing?"

"Sleeping."

"You up for company?"

Does it really matter what I say? "Yeah that's cool," I answer. I give him my address and tell him to call me from my corner as my door doesn't have a buzzer. He says he would be right over. I jump in the shower and put away my porn magazines; I am just throwing my dirty socks into the hamper when my phone rings again. I let him in and he take a look around my apartment and meets my roommate.

When we get to the kitchen I offer him something to drink. He declined, and after shuffling his feet a little he suggests we go to my bedroom. He sits in my desk chair and before I can take a seat he says he changed his mind and wants a glass of water. I go to the kitchen, wash a glass out of the pile of dirty dishes. When I return to my bedroom he is taking off his boots. I put the glass on the desk in front of him and flop on my bed.

To my surprise he downs the water and asks me for another glass. I do not know what he is up to, but it's hard to refuse a guest. So I comply, and when I returned to the bedroom he is sitting with his shirt off, his baseball cap still on, and his pants unbuttoned. We kiss, and I rub his chest and I wonder if he might be the next one, the one to make me feel like I shouldn't be fucking anyone else. I take off my shirt and he is licking my nipple, suddenly moving down my side to my navel, and then unbuckling my belt.

His name is Oscar, I remember as he is going down on me, and he is not Spanish but since he grew up with a lot of Puerto Rican neighbours he is thus racially indistinct – kind of dark and shady with an elusive edge. If grungy were a race he would win the pageant.

My pants are down around my ankles and I am closing my eyes. I am enjoying the blow job when suddenly, he picks up the half glass of water and downs it. He holds it up with a smile. I smile back thinking, I bet he's not the one. I fetch the water and he's back on my dick again. I have seen him around enough to think that he won't try anything too terribly wrong; my misguided notion of human nature at the time leads me to believe that crime of course only happens between total strangers.

I'm thinking something is wrong, but what could it be. Certainly I have no idea what could be wrong. I decide to strike out in uncharted waters and see what obstacles there are. I lay Oscar back on the bed and lean beside him. We kiss, and I reach down his pants where his limp dick is waiting patiently for me. I massage him slowly, and it starts to enlarge slightly, not exactly getting hard but at least coming out of its slumber. Our tongues are swabbing and our bodies pressed tight against each other; this seems to be acceptable.

I go down on Oscar. The worst thing that happens is that he seems uncertain of where to put his hands. At first they are on my head, then my back, grabbing my shoulders, above his head. There is no way that he will become comfortable. His crotch smells like soap but I can't quite place the brand. This is uncomfortable, but it still seems within acceptable boundaries. His dick won't get hard. He's scared, or high, or maybe even straight. These are not

Mind Over Matter

problems, simply conditions. What then is the problem?

"My back hurts," Oscar says. His eyes are open. His hand have landed on the side, near his hips.

"Why does it hurt?" I ask. What was I supposed to say?

"I dunno." He wiggles his legs, and I get out of the way so that he can roll over. I guess I am to rub his back until it feels better. I rub it and he complains, "Not there." I am on his shoulders, so I move down.

"Here?"

"No, that part feels fine." I move down some more. I am starting to get the idea. The mid part of his back doesn't get a response; in the small of his back he says, "No, lower." There is nowhere to go but his ass. This is all a cheap ploy isn't it. I rub his cheeks and he wiggles a little. He has crossed his arms and buried his head. I wonder if his back really hurts, but soon I am not worried about his aching muscles as an aching part of my body instead has attracted my attention.

"Do you want me to get a condom?" He doesn't actually say anything, just lets out an affirmative grunt. Condoms are kept in a convenient nearby location and I am soon wearing one, with some greasy enabler on my finger. I explore his ass with a clean finger and, once I know where the hole is, follow it with the lube. He may not have been expecting that; it was kind of chilled and maybe he is more used to a little spit and a deep breath. He settles down though and soon enough my finger is met with little resistance.

My dick, however, was a different matter entirely. Technically there should be nothing wrong, as his ass is primed. But while some guys hate fingers or anything artificial but can take any size dick, other guys love fingers and dildoes but a dick makes them close right up. He is the latter. I am on his back with my dick against his hole, and is was no hope for me. I reach down to find out what was the matter, and it seems to be the same way since last I was there. Puzzled, I get my dick up in there and tried it again.

"Does it hurt?" I ask. Maybe he's in pain but doesn't want to say anything.

"No, it's not bothering me at all." That is tantamount to asking me to try harder. Reaching down I spread out his ass and let my dick push into its hole. I strain as much as I can, and suddenly I am in. He must have been fronting, because once I was there, there was plenty of room. His ass is warm and strong. Every time I rest he squeezes me, and when I'm cumming he massages my dick until the last drops are out.

Wouldn't you know it, after I have rolled to the side and have barely gotten the jimmy off he is asking for more water. Something is wrong, very wrong. I pull on a stray pair of shorts and fill the glass for the last time. He asks me to call him a car service to take him to his sister's apartment. Sure why not, I think. We go downstairs to wait. Oscar smiles and turns away from the street, and facing my building takes a long, full piss.

My company is concerned enough that I get to work at midnight that it sends a car service to pick me up. I've tried every night for the entire eight months that I've worked there to bag one of the drivers, to no avail. It seems like such a natural thing – Good evening, Mr. Leslie, why don't you come sit in the front seat? What radio station would you like to listen to? How about we turn off onto this side street and you show me what it's like to be satisfied by another man?

Sometimes a driver will start to talk about a few of my fellow employees, and by piecing together office gossip and the occasional flirtation, I start to wonder if the drivers get it on with the closet gays in my office and I don't get any simply because I'm not closeted enough. But instead of worrying I prefer to lean back in the Lincoln's leather seats and stroke my dick absently as the driver brings me to work, waiting for the day that something will happen. I look into the rear-view mirror regularly, and sometimes the driver is looking back, but that's as far as it ever goes.

The building where I work has twenty-four hour security, and they used to give me trouble when I tried to get in. I can't blame them. I'm not sure what I'd think if I saw some kid with baggy, baggy jeans, baseball caps, bright shirts, and a heavy black coat in the winter. Big black shoes, or bright white sneakers. A fade, facial hair. Black knapsack. Not someone who should be walking freely around in this office building.

I was doing the street thing long before I started working there, so I can't say that I do it as a rebellion against my corporate identity. But I have to say that all the confusion I cause has, at least, given me satisfaction when I do it well. They used to stop me, trying to tell me that messengers have to go in

Mind Over Matter

through the side, sign in on the fifteenth floor, call up to the office first, et cetera. And then I'd tell them I work here, and show them my identification. They'd scowl, realising that not only do I work in a stuffy corporate office, but that I don't run errands or sort mail. They'd look at me and see a street kid, a boy from the boroughs, and then they see my identification and discover that I'm working a pussy office job. I'm in the same class as the suits that yell at them if there's garbage in the elevator trash can, or if they fall asleep, or for no reason at all.

I've always been disappointed that we don't have a cute security guard. There is a new guy with a big butt working there, on Wednesday and Thursday nights. He's kind of geeky and cute. He always smiles and chatters nervously when I come in. Last week he cut his hair off, buzzing it down to an eighth of an inch like mine, and made a point of saying that now we look like brothers. He leaves me alone as I wait for the elevator. I wonder what it would be like to have sex with him. My hand is already on my dick – it's been there since I got out of the car – and I start to rub it.

I totally could pull off the straight-boy act with him. Talk to him a little every night, asking him his name and where he lives and how long he's been a security guard and stuff. And then one night, on my way out to lunch, I'll stop and talk to him for a longer time, about nothing. I'll have my hand on my crotch, and let him try not to look as my dick gets hard and starts to poke through my jeans.

Why don't you sit on that chair? I lead him over to the chair he brings out and sit him down on it. I stand before him, my crotch in his face, and wait for a minute. I'd rather have him unzip my pants and take out my dick, but he's too nervous and certainly not adventurous enough to do that, so I unbuckle my pants and slide them down. He reaches up and touches it, looking at me, shaking slightly. I pull it out of my underwear and lean forward, putting it into his mouth. He hesitates at first, then sucks it down. Take off your shirt, I tell him, and he quickly pulls it off. His chest is sort of hairy, and he has a little bit of a belly, but I close my eyes and feel his naked arms against my thighs and am lost in his sucking.

The doors to the elevator finally open, and take me up to the nineteenth floor. Let's get in the elevator, I tell him. No, not that one. Over here. I lead him to an express elevator that goes to the top of the building, forty-eight floors. I get in and punch the button for the top floor. I touch him on his shoulders and he gets on his knees. He takes my dick, still poking out of my pants, into his mouth, and sucks me all the way to the top. I have grabbed on to the aluminum rail and leaned my head against the fake wood paneling. When I look up I can see the guy sucking my dick in the polished brass. This is where it's at, and even though the ride to the top of the building is relatively short I'm already ready to cum.

The doors open on a the foyer of a closed office. I pull him off my dick and hold the doors open with my foot. Take off your pants. The guy hesitates, and then complies. Your underwear, too. I turn him around and he grabs on to the rail. I punch the button for the lobby and as the doors close I spit on my dick. It slides easily into his asshole, and I fuck him, quickly and with a force, as we fall forty-eight stories to the ground floor.

The doors open on the lobby and I shoot my load, and then tell him, "Thanks," and that I'll see him later. As I walk away, I hope that he's a little bewildered, naked and covered with cum, with an aching hard-on.

I've been sitting at work for almost an hour, typesetting a hideous chart that seems to show the breakdown of expected and actual returns for six different divisions over the past seven years. In the fluorescent light and sterile air of the office I'm suddenly conscious of my odour; the T-shirt I've been wearing this week under other (clean) shirts smells like smoke and sex. A faint odour rises from my shoes, which I haven't washed in a while. And, worst of all, I have the smell of butt on my fingers and my face from a guy who I had sex with at the video store on the way to work. I don't think anyone has noticed – at night, the employees sit kind of far from each other – but I decide to go clean up a little.

The bathroom, as always, is empty. I carefully wash my hands and face with the pink, sweet-smelling liquid soap, and run water through the stubble on my head. I wipe off with paper towels, and save one damp one to wipe off my armpits and my crotch. As I'm swabbing my dick I notice a red bump at the base of my shaft. Adrenaline shoots through my body as I think that I have herpes or something, but it looks more like a common pimple. Most likely it's a friction blister from jerking off. Actually, from its position way down on my

Mind Over Matter

shaft, it's probably a dried-up blood blister from sticking my dick through the glory holes in the peep booths on Third and Fourteenth Street. My head is spinning, going through every possible explanation as I push my pubic hair out of the way to and lean out of the light to get a better look.

I haven't clipped my fingernails in a while, and I use the sharp points on my thumb and forefinger to lance it. It doesn't come off at first and pain shoots through my groin as the growth, or scab, or whatever it is, swells. Suddenly it pops and blood squirts. I look at the offensive cells in the light; it's a small, flat disc of hardened flesh. Just a cyst, I suppose, as I flick it into the urinal and flush. I take off my denim shirt and T-shirt. I decide that the best I can do is put the offending T-shirt in my backpack and zip it up tight to hide the odour.

I put my denim shirt back on, feeling a little sleazy without a T-shirt. I look down and a nickel-sized stain of blood has soaked into my white boxer shorts. I walk to the sink and wash off my dick, getting the boy's cum and my blood and the general funk off. I dry off with paper towels and inspect the wound; already it has closed up to a tiny pin-prick of red. Just to be sure, I open the medicine cabinet under the sink and pour a little rubbing alcohol on it, which stings pleasantly for a good half hour.

I go back to my work space and throw my T-shirt into my backpack, drawing a questioning, or knowing, glance from the hip woman that sits next to me. I shrug my shoulders and get back to work. The associate that has given me this horrendous chart was in the office yesterday morning when I left for home, and he's still here now. He comes in to check on my progress and I see how tired he is. Have you been here since this morning. He nods his head. These boys really work themselves to death. Just two weeks ago, he passed out in the middle of the day, right in front of one of the firm's officers, and had to go to the hospital. Instead of resting, though, he decided to work even harder after that. Don't want anyone to think that he's not up to the job, of course. Fucking crazy.

I notice that he's wearing a different shirt and tie, though. He must keep a store of them in his office. I know that there is a shower upstairs, but I didn't think that anyone actually used it. "Why don't you go home and get some rest? This will be done by six, and you can come in and look it over before your meeting." He looks at his watch and considers it. "I can call you to wake you up if you want." That settles it. He looks relieved as he gives me his home phone number, says thanks and walks out.

At three-thirty in the morning, halfway through my shift, it's time for lunch. There is some film that need to be processed for a presentation the next day, so I pull them out of the imager and write up the work order. The all-night company we use for processing is just a few blocks away, and I decide to go for a walk and drop them off.

The building where I have to leave the film has a kind of crazy doorman who's always asking me about my girlfriends. I ignore him, cruelly, to the point of being an asshole, but still he won't let up. I drop off the film and look at my watch. I have twenty-five minutes before my break is over. Instead of getting something to eat, I decide to walk up to Second Avenue to this diner which has a really cute guy who cleans up, starting at three in the morning.

I first saw him one night before I started working at my present job. I had heard that this area, near Rounds, was rife with prostitutes. I still haven't seen any, but when I was walking around I did see this boy through the window. He was mopping the floor in the front of the diner.

The boy stopped mopping and watched me as I walked by, so when I got to the next corner I turned around and went back. I stood near the windows for awhile, checking him out. He looked young, but was certainly old enough. I immediately found him attractive and started stroking my dick. He was kind of short and skinny. A Mexican guy with jet-black hair, cut short on top with a length in the back tied into a ponytail. He was wearing a cleaner's uniform, all white, and had rolled up the cuffs of its pants to reveal his calves. As I watched he took off his shirt, and I had quite a show watching this half-naked, sweaty guy clean. He finished moping, and then started to go over the areas he'd already mopped. When he came close to where I was standing, I could see that he wasn't wearing any underwear, and his pubic hair made a dark patch on the stained white work pants.

I watched for at least ten minutes as he re-mopped the floor, watching me slyly. When he finished he sat down in a booth near a window. I took that as an invitation, so I walked over and unzipped my coat, letting him watch as I touched my stiff cock through my jeans. This freaked him out. He stood up

Mind Over Matter

and started giving me as much attitude as he could, being that he was a lot smaller than me and separated from me, by glass. He put his shirt back on and made menacing motions, and was shouting something that I couldn't make out. I didn't know what had happened, but I certainly wasn't out to piss him off, so I shrugged my shoulders and walked off.

I had been up there a few times since, and each time he ignored me for awhile before getting pissed off again. But since his initial reaction had been so good, I figured that he just got scared. As I walk up Second Avenue, I wonder what it would take to get him to relax. A light bulb goes off over my head, and I decide I will offer him twenty dollars. That should be enough, I suppose. Not spare change, but not so extravagant that I can't do it again. I don't want to offend him by offering him too little, but I'm not exactly made of money, either.

This time, I'm going to walk right up to the glass. He'll come over and start to yell, and I'll unfold the bill onto the glass. He'll look at if for a minute, and then give me a puzzled look. I'll point as his crotch, and then rub mine. He'll get the idea. He'll come over to where I'm standing, rubbing his dick. I'll motion with my hand, and he'll take his dick out of his pants and jerk off for me. I'll do the same. We'll continue that way until someone walks by. We'll zip up nervously, and when the pedestrian is gone I'll motion to the back door and walk over. I'll wait outside for an uncomfortable time while he decides if he wants to take the risk of letting me in. Finally, his hard dick will decide for him, and he'll let me in.

From the street I can see the kitchen, and that's where we'll go. I'll hand him the twenty dollars, which he'll stick on the counter. Then I'll pull down his pants and help him up onto the long, cold aluminum table. He'll sit with his legs dangling over the edge, his pants around his ankles. I'll suck him off, holding his hands to his sides, making him concentrate on getting his dick sucked. When he gets close to cumming he'll struggle, and I'll let him push me away. He'll get up on all fours and stick his butt in my face. I'll eat out his ass as he jerks off, moaning, and he'll shoot his load on the counter, his ass muscles twitching around my tongue. When he's finished, I'll kiss him, no tongue, on the lips, and give him a quick hug before taking off. I won't come back for a few weeks after that, and then show up when he's given up on ever seeing me again.

I'm all ready to do it when I get there. I walk up to the diner and the floor's already mopped. I peer through the window, and the boy is washing dishes in the kitchen. When he looks up he sees me, yells something, and slams the door. I shrug my shoulders and look at the time: I've got ten minutes to get back to work. I don't want to abuse my lunch time – I decided shortly after I started working there that the key is to do exactly what is asked of me, very well, and not to abuse anything so that they'll leave me alone. It's worked so far, so I hop into a cab and got back to work five minutes early, disappointed and horny.

I stop at the 24-hour store on the corner near where I work. I don't have any money. Which is really strange since I just got paid the day before. I should have 100 dollars in my wallet. There isn't anything. Did I forget and deposit my whole pay check? Unlikely. Did I walk away from the bank leaving the money behind? Even less likely. Did I make a fool out of myself obeying that punk Oscar's endless requests for water? Very likely.

Well the next time I meet Oscar I will be hanging out at the peep show that I pass to and from work. This is some time later and I am not immediately thinking of the money I lost. I mean, I did not actually see him take it, and my roommate could just as easily had lifted it as well. While he has stolen from me before, the booty has mostly been sandwich meat and prepared food; most times he fesses up after his crimes even though he doesn't try to make amends. And maybe he knew I was getting paid today, and let word slip to someone else he was acquainted with who decided it was a good opportunity. But still, jumping to immediate judgments is not exactly my style. And besides, you don't let guys in your apartment without accepting some risk.

I have seen Oscar several times that night. He is smiling at me every time we catch each others' eye. At one point he came out of a booth after some older man who did not look very happy. After he has cleared out Oscar asks me if I want to go out for a smoke so we are standing on the street.

I am checking the kid out, remembering how cute he is. He is all dressed up like he was going somewhere or had been somewhere. He wears all the right street labels, a print shirt and shorts that ended below his knees, hiking boots, a real nicely dressed hood with a slim gold chain. Funny, I don't know

Mind Over Matter

him to wear jewellery – especially since he can't boost it. Robbing jewellery stores is a serious business. I stare at it, feeling again like something was wrong but not sure what. He sees me staring and, suddenly, we come to the realisation simultaneously: Oscar had stolen the chain from me, probably when I was filling up his glass. And it had been long enough before and intervening events had masked the fact from both of us, until we were there standing on the street having a smoke.

I had had a feeling that he had cleaned out my wallet, but I certainly was not sure, and then there was the evidence around his neck. Oscar clutches at the chain with a look of shock, and then starts trying to bust the fuck out of there. I grab his arm and push him over a nearby car, causing the alarm to sound. Those fuckers are loud when you're standing right next to them, so I am shouting to be heard. "You motherfucker don't you think I won't crack your fucking head open. I'm gonna tell you just once to stay the fuck outta here. Cause I hang with some real horny bastards that would really love a bitch-assed punk like you. You hear me?" I bang his head onto the hood for emphasis, and then bring his arm up behind his back, pinning him so he wouldn't try anything.

"It's a shame you didn't work out," I whisper in his ear as I undo the clasp of Oscar's chain – I mean, my chain – with my right hand. "Cause you got a real nice punk ass." He stays quiet, which makes me kind of nervous. I didn't know him to pack heat, but there was no way to worry about that now. I release his arm and walk off slowly, to show that I wasn't afraid.

The morning crew is coming in as I finish up my last assignment of the day. I am slightly distracted by my imagination but it isn't anything serious. I don't have much time to think about anything until after I leave for the day. Given the hour you would think there is nothing going on but you would be wrong. While the work day proper hasn't even started, already there are crises all around. I ask the morning supervisor if he needs help, but he says they've got it under control so I get out of there before someone mistakes me for someone who is still on the clock.

I am thinking about my violent thoughts toward Oscar and my eyes are misting a little, the violent daydream recalling my first fight – I was off visiting my cousins, and this punk they knew from school came riding up with a few friends and started causing trouble. I was young, but I don't know what age I was. Somewhere around ten I suppose. And so this kid comes up, looking for trouble, and we all waited for someone to do something about it.

Finally the kid settled on me, I guess because I was the biggest, and we fell to a fist fight. I got hit once in the stomach but mostly I was doing the punching, and soon the kid was lying on the sandy ground. "Have you had enough?" I said, out of breath, leaning over and holding out my hand to help him up. As a response he cracked me in the nose, hard, and continued to fight. I don't remember how it finally ended, but the kid eventually ended up running off and I was a hero for a day.

I didn't feel very heroic, though. As soon as the kid had pedalled off, I ran to my grandmother's garage and started to cry. My eldest cousin thought I was hurt and went to find my parents, but I was just bawling out of shame. My parents and my uncle came in frantic and, once determining that there was nothing broken, heard the story from someone. I was just crying and crying, snot dripping out of my nose and everything. It was quite a mess. Finally my uncle made the prognosis that the only thing that had been hurt was my pride and told everybody to leave me alone.

For the rest of the night, it seemed like every time I dried up someone would say something that would upset me, something about how I had given that kid a beating or what a troublemaker he was, and I would start to bawl again, leaving behind a confused relative asking, "What did I say? Look, Chris, I'm sorry," as I ran to the garage. And even today if I think too long of shaking in my father's arms, bawling uncontrollably, him stroking my hair, I get tears in my eyes. Kinda fucked up, right?

I'm not much of a fighter, and rarely seem to get into trouble. Which is why I don't have scars littering my face, scalp and hands – and while my lack of battle scars is sometimes a feature, sometimes I am told by someone in a fit of anger that they want to cut my virgin skin. But in the few times I've been called on to defend myself, I've been able to do it. I learned a long time ago that despite the fact that boys claim to be accomplished fighters, when it comes down to it no one really knows what they are doing. It doesn't take any special skill to win a fight, just the ability to cling to your courage and finding

Mind Over Matter

the right moment to walk away. And even the hardest boy needs to go off and hide after a fight, even if he is the victor.

After a few blocks I had pretty much dried up. I wonder at what had just happened. The recurring bouts of crying that night with my cousins were like ripples in the pond; and now some twenty years later another ripple had broken the surface. I snap out of it and find myself staring in the face of this proto-banjee teenager who had been watching my progress up the street. Guess it's not every day you see a guy openly crying on the street. I walk by feeling vaguely embarrassed but soon he is behind me.

I think the mini-encounter is over but then, the teen-ager calls after me. "Yo, B." I turned to look him in the face, my eyes still red and moist. He doesn't know what to say but he wants say something. "Don't let them get you down, alright?" he says finally. "It'll be okay tomorrow."

I head west to Eighth Avenue, on my way to one of my favourite peep shows near Thirty-Fourth Street. I slink along the storefronts until I reach the building. Once inside I go straight to the bathroom, not wanting to see anyone, and wash my face. I am thinking to myself that I should have just made that fucker, cause I knew I could have beaten the shit out of him. That kid's probably taking in more money than I am, and he gets off taking shit from me. That's fucked up. I shrug my shoulders in the mirror and give myself a real long look.

Feeling slightly better I change a twenty for ten ones and two fives, attracting the attention of several nearby hustlers. I ignore them, since they're mostly zooted and therefore no good to me – once the initial thrill wears off, who wants to pay ten dollars to suck on a limp dick?

I decide that this morning to be gay and head behind the beaded curtain to the gay booths, ignore the older patrons and the younger hustlers and find a clean booth. I slip two dollars into the slot and select my favourite movie of the moment, a "lockup" film. It's been playing there for weeks, and I can't see enough of it.

It finally comes, the scene where the dark, large-dicked "prison guard" lectures the cute, young "prisoner" about his crimes. He tells him that if he doesn't watch out for him, he can make his time in prison real tough. The young prisoner, of course, wants to make his time as soft as possible, and a run-of-the-mill blow job follows. But then the security guard tires of the sucking and lies down, on his back, and pulls the prisoner on top of him, back down. The security guard's long, fat dick is instantly in the ass of the skinny, smaller prisoner, and I watch as the prisoner jerks off his little dick as the big-dicked guard slides in and out of his ass.

My dick is rock hard, and my two dollars have run out. I open the door to the booth and nearly hit this old businessman type in the face; he was trying to get a look through the crack in the door. I scowl at him and walk around the corner, looking to see who's there.

Aside from the businessmen on the way to work, who always seem to hang out there for a few minutes without doing anything, there were a few hustlers. One of them I knew before; I met him around Christmas-time, his opening line was that he hated the holidays because he never gets any presents. I told him I wasn't buying and he went away. I saw him a few weeks later, in January, and he admired my new shirt. I stupidly told him that it was a Christmas gift from my sister, thus giving him the opportunity to bemoan the fact that he had not gotten anything. He went on for awhile, but then he must have realised that I wasn't feeling sorry for him because he then he switched the story slightly and said that his mother had bought him a new pair of sneakers. "Moms are good for that," he said.

The next time I saw him, he told me that I was looking really good and asked me what I got into. I told him I was looking to get my dick sucked. He told me he would suck it good, not like these other guys that just pretended for a while and then made you pay, anyway. For just ten dollars, he said, he would give me the best blow I had ever had. I told him no, because if it's only worth ten dollars I was not interested. But asked me to think about it, since he could really use the money.

The next time I saw him, I did it. He was right, he really turned me out. I didn't have to do anything, and he was grateful for the cash. I walk over and ask him what's up, he says hello and, as usual, tells me that I look good. I walk into a booth and he follows, no need to talk about any arrangements. I give him his due and he gives me mine, and in three dollars (twelve minutes) we're done. I leave first, sweaty and somewhat dishevelled, and he waits for the next opportunity.

IN THE PITTS
by Michael Lassell

Okay, so first I should tell you that I'm not rich – not by a butt-fucking long shot. Thanks to the vagaries of New York City real-estate law, however, not to mention rent-control loopholes (legal and not) and a bit of palm-greasing, I live in a luxury building in a scummy "gentrifying" neighbourhood on the river (Hudson, lower). It's the kind of building where it would not, in fact, be all that unusual to run into Brad Pitt strutting out of the elevator into the lobby.

I mean, Linda Evangelista (I'm told) has a place here because it's close to Industria, the hipper-than-dykes-on-TV photo studio, and Drew Barrymore, too, when she's working in town. Everyone feels paternal to Drew, for some reason—probably related to how helpless she always seems, fame and fortune notwithstanding. She'll come home in a black stretch limo after a long day's work and sit on the front steps dishing with all the gay boys on rollerblades and their winded dogs, and everyone will go *"Awwww!"* like she's a three-year-old taking her first step.

So I was kind of surprised just how surprised I actually was the afternoon I walked through the lobby of my very own building and Brad himself stepped out of the elevator, a cigarette half hidden in the cup of his hand, head sort of bowed, looking out from underneath his eyebrows the way he does as if to say, "Oh, I'm sorry, but let's be real, I'm Brad Pitt for Chrissake, and I can smoke anywhere I want."

Normally I think people who smoke should have their lips sewn shut, and that was the first thing I thought when this tall blond hunk sort of slunk past me knowing he was *not* supposed to be smoking in an elevator – at least not in New York in 1997 – but going right ahead and doing it nonetheless. It took me about one half a New York nanosecond to clock this number as my No.1 cinematic heartthrob in all his semi-shaved pseudo-scruffy glory. So he was smoking. I could die of lung cancer happy if it came from the noxious molecules of Brad Pitt's regurgitated toxic fumes. Okay, I'm lying. I'd sue.

Now, I am not generally a star-fucker, except for the stars I've actually fucked (names available on request), but I fell in love with Brad Pitt's flawlessly unpitted butt in *Thelma and Louise*, and I've been faithful ever since, even though I know this makes me a late-comer to the Brad-wagon, and I have to admit that lately I've gotten kind of tired of his talking with the corners of his mouth pinched together all the time. I mean, who doesn't love a coy smirk and a shy shuffle? But he's 31, for Chrissake! Or 32. I forget.

It's the long-haired Pitt of the early mid-'90s that cooks my chili low and slow, which means, Brad B.G. ("Before Gwyneth"). You know: the tortured Louis Pointe du Lac in *Interview with the Vampire* (at the moment his lips come within striking distance of Tom Cruise's lips) and Tristan (be still my heart) in *Legends of the Fall*, which should have won the Golden Globe, I don't care what anybody says. Who the fuck do those foreign journalists think they are? They are *guests* in this country after all.

Yes, I'm a sucker for pain. I just *love* that wounded, tortured, introspective thing our Bradley does with those baby blues. Actually, of course, he's kind of dumb in real life, which I suppose could turn me off in other circumstances. I mean, who but a moron could actually say *Baywatch* was his favourite TV program? – not to mention that he hangs out at Hogs & Heifers, a biker bar that was putrid enough when it was just an actual hetero biker bar, and is now beyond tolerance since it was "discovered" by Hollywood hunklets with image problems. And NYU undergraduates, for Chrissake, who, by the way, jump out of their pimply skins and piss themselves if you so much as glower at them on the street, which I do whenever I see one slumming the Meat Packing District, where things are *way* too public these days.

Anyway, it's the long-haired Brad that reminds me of the days when everyone had hair that long (although most of us didn't bleach ours), the days before everything was so complicated and boys who loved boys just mellowed into each other's arms for an hour or a week or a lifetime. It is not the long-haired Godiva Brad, however, who saunters out of my Otis special (maximum capacity 9000 pounds), but the millennial, less hirsute but still stubbly incarnation, sort of a cross between David Mills at the end of *Se7en* and IRA

In The Pitts

Rory (a.k.a. Frankie the Angel) in _The Devil's Own_ (but after he cut off the beard).

And the boy – thank God – is tall. Most of 'em are way shorter than they look on screen. William Bradley Pitt of Shawnee, Oklahoma, is every inch of five-foot-eleven (his official height), but I'd believe six, six-one no problem – at least in cowboy boots, which he wears, which can be a turn-on (sometimes) – especially if I am looking up (and I was).

I got to my apartment – way out of breath – and pushed the intercom, a frequently futile gesture.

"Front desk..." an answer crackled.

God was on my side.

"Art," I gushed, "who was that who just left the building?"

"Oh, Spike..." he moaned, knowing he shouldn't say. But Art can't lie, at least to me. Like the time I came in and said, "Who's the big shot tonight?" because there were three white vans parked out front, and Art said, "The mayor, but don't tell anyone I told you."

(If it was supposed to be a low-profile visit, Hizzoner probably shouldn't have parked three Secret Service vehicles directly in front of the revolving door, I remember thinking, but the mayor is, if nothing else, IQ-impaired.)

"Art," I said, my voice growing insistent, "I have not had a good day, not a good day at all, and I am _not_ in the mood for games. Now you know I love you, so: Was that Brad Pitt?"

Unsurprisingly, my favourite doorman chose the low road and caved: "He's moving in, but don't tell anyone I told you."

It appeared those Gwyneth Paltrow splitsville rumours were a bit more than idle gossip (for this was _weeks_ before the little blond salt-and-peppershaker studio darlings announced their "amicable separation").

"Penthouse 9?" I whispered hoarsely into the static-plagued intercom.

"Spiiiiiiiike...," Art whined.

Like it could be any place else. Nine was the 3-bedroom palazzo recently vacated by a certain opera-loving bachelor Republican, a significant contributor to the last mayoral campaign, and the man the mayor used to visit here, until this neighbour nobody seemed to know suddenly came up not living here anymore about the same time the mayor's wife and son moved out of Gracie Mansion in the most under-reported news story of the year.

"Forget it," I said, thinking I'd have to up Art's Christmas tip, and I ran to my dresser and pulled out the keys to Penthouse 8, where a couple of lesbian friends of mine lived when they were in town, which was almost never, and I had their keys in case of an emergency – like when I needed to sunbathe on their terrace.

I ran to the elevator, put the special PH key in the special PH lock and turned it to the right. Up Mr. Elevator climbed.

The top floor was ghostly quiet. Partly because no one who owned one of these huge places actually lived in them. They were places to *have*, not *homes* to live in. They were 'in-town' places. Overnighters. High-class fuck-pads.

I put my ear up to the door of No. 8. The girls were out. And, they were, believe me – since before Ellen DeGeneres was born. If they'd been home, Atilla the Yorkie would've been shrieking like a banshee with a hot poker up her derriere. A *Yorkie*, for Chrissake! No wonder I didn't know they were queer until I saw them liplocked in the laundry room the first time, getting hot while their undies were in the dyer. (Now, *men* with Yorkies I'd have known.)

My heart was pounding in my ears as I stepped up to No. 9 and listened to the silence behind the door. I put my cheek to the mustard-yellow metal Brad had recently closed behind him and could practically feel his dimples on my cheek. I couldn't resist: I put my hand on the knob he had turned with his muscular hands. I, too, turned the knob. Miracle! It rotated to the right, the latch let loose, and the door swung heavily inward.

I gasped. I thought my liver, or at least my pancreas, would blob out of my body, my insides were so shaken.

I looked both ways down the hall, stepped inside, closed the door behind me, and locked it as quietly as I could, which wasn't very, (reinforced-steel New York apartment doors being what they are).

There I stood, alone with 3,500 hundred square feet of refinished oak floor. I was a pillar of unexamining desire in a wilderness of Navajo White. (The "natural charm" of the place you could read about later in *Metropolitan Home* came, in fact, from a million dollars' worth of highly contrived interior

In The Pitts

design.)

The place was totally, absolutely, finally, and deafeningly empty. Except for a half-empty bottle of Corona Extra on the white Formica kitchen counter. Or was it half-full?

What a perfect white-boy drink, I remember thinking, as I zeroed in on the honey-coloured, amber-hued, kinky-sex-tinted liquid sitting there in its pillar of clear glass.

I squinted it into full focus. I circled it, watching it like a rustler a rattler. Finally, I touched it, gently, to see if the puppy was dead. It was still cool, still 'sweating.' I put my fingers around it's throat and lifted it to my face. I sniffed its open end. I read the label–the *whole* label:

Corona ® Extra. LA CERVEZA MAS FINA MADE IN MEXICO MARC.REG. BEER. 12 FL. OZ. Brewed and bottled by CERVECERIA MODELO, S.A. DE C.V. MEXICO, D.F. REG. S.S.A. No 7417 'B.' And the back, too: IMPORTED BY THE GAMBRINUS COMPANY SAN ANTONIO, TEXAS 78232 U.S.A. **GOVERNMENT WARNING**: (1) ACCORDING TO THE SURGEON GENERAL, WOMEN SHOULD NOT DRINK ALCOHOLIC BEVERAGES DURING PREGNANCY BECAUSE OF THE RISK OF BIRTH DEFECTS. (2) CONSUMPTION OF ALCOHOLIC BEVERAGES IMPAIRS YOUR ABILITY TO DRIVE A CAR OR OPERATE MACHINERY, AND MAY CAUSE HEALTH PROBLEMS. MA - CT - ME - VT - DE - NY 5¢ REFUND. There was a striped bar code, too, which was numbered: 0 806614 5. I'd have read the cap, but it wasn't there.

Of course, 'label' isn't, maybe, the right term, not exactly, since the good folks at Corona have the extraordinary good sense to stamp their 'label' directly onto the bottle, not to some glued-up patch of identification that is 'affixed' mechanically and after the fact of filling. That Corona label was fused or etched or whatever the word is right onto the glass. Very neat in a beer bottle, more than effective. I figured Brad had bought the brew at the corner 'Gourmet Deli' and left the cap behind when they popped it for him.

I put the glass of its long tapered neck to my mouth and ran my tongue around it, as if were the tight virgin asshole of a teenager intent on losing his cherry. I tilted it back and let some of the leftover liquid run into my throat. It was beer, all right, and Brad's beer at that–some of it possibly washed back out of his throat, past those pouty female lips and Colgate teeth.

That's when the idea hit.

I yanked the door open and flew down the hall to the elevator. I punched the down button, waiting, waiting.... "Fuuuuuck," I said to myself under my breath. Okay, it wasn't under my breath. And, besides, who had any breath left?

In my apartment, I dashed over to the computer, punched it on and, while it was whirring itself into existence, I ripped off my clothes and pulled on my baggiest pair of shorts and loosest T.

I punched some buttons on the keyboard and waited, screaming obscenities at AOL while the system limped into action. Finally, I got the gif I wanted and punched the PRINT button–set for 200 percent, of course.

Thank God the image was in black and white, because I was going crazy, pulling on my dick, first through the thin plaid of my cotton shorts, then up one leg, my dick stiff in my hand while Brad Pitt, naked as a jay bird, his own lovely and perhaps semi-hard dick bouncing under his Greek statue of a torso, came rolling out of my printer. (I'd have come on the keys before his belly button showed up if this thing was trying to print in colour). Okay, so it was a bad print of a stolen newspaper image I'd copped from the Internet. But it was my Brad–thank you Jesus and the sleaze-bag paparazzi of Europe! – and he was just how I wanted him (naked and defenseless against my elaborate demands on his comely flesh).

I grabbed the grease from the night-table drawer, yanked the Scotch tape from the dispenser on my desk and went back upstairs.

Inside Brad's new apartment, I shed my clothes in a tug and a shrug, ran to the obviously remodelled master bathroom, turned on the tap in the glass-in shower, then ran back to the kitchen and grabbed the Corona bottle. I chugged what liquid was left and took my rare and valuable, now empty, relic to the bathroom.

I taped the picture of Brad up on one side of the shower, above the splash zone, and I let the hot water of Brad's shower pour over me.

I ran my hands on every part of myself, but mostly, of course, the 'special' places forbidden to children. I was a cock from head to foot and I was strokin'

In The Pitts

hard, imagining every part of Brad in my mouth, imagining my tongue on his six-pack abs and across his nipples (the kind so flat they seem like little sunken craters with Indian burial grounds erect in their centres). And his dick – his thick, cut, hard as rock 'n' roll, pumping, throbbing pound of mandrake flesh – I could almost feel it in my throat it was so real to me.

I dropped down to the floor of the shower, put my legs on the wall just under Brad's dear, sweet, purloined Internet image and opened the phallic plastic container of lube and stuck a wad of it up my ass. Then I kissed the mouth of the beer bottle one more time and touched its now-warm orifice to my ready, willing, and able asshole.

"Lick it, Brad," I said as I rubbed it around my asshole, the sphincter practically puckering to take it in. Then began to push. "Fuck me, baby," I said, "Fuck me like you never fucked a man before." The head of the bottle was less problem than an average male thumb, and after that it was fairly clear sailing. I pushed that long-necked bottle past its slightly swelling bulge and gave my asshole a rest at the slight indentation below it where the body of the bottle starts. I thought the body of the bottle would be a challenge, but that little baby (okay more than a baby, a well-developed adolescent, and probably bigger than Brad himself) slipped in so far I had to stop before I lost it in wet velvet folds.

I could feel the tip of the bottle against that prostrate button I have come to love and was groaning loud enough to make the bathroom echo. I felt my asshole open up like the mouth of a whale in a school of sea lions.

I fucked myself silly with the bottle thinking all the time I'd manage to break it on the tile floor and rip myself open, thinking that someone might come in—the super, the painters, or Brad himself, alone or with friends. But I didn't stop. I pushed *la cerveza de mi coraz w* in far enough to cross home plate, then pulled it into the outfield, pushed it in and pulled it nearly out, my hands as slippery as the greasy glass. I had to close my eyes, where the visuals were tight-torso Brad shoving that photogenic torpedo of his in and out of my butt and then–reverse angle!–I'd be fucking him, his well-carved head rolling back and forth on the pillow of his (okay bleached) blond hair (it *could* have been the Montana sun).

I folded my tongue into a roll so it would feel more like Brad's cock in my mouth, and I dug my fingernails into my own dick and balls pretending the hot scrape came from Brad's three-day growth of beard, then picturing his ruby-red rectal verandah open to the breeze, ready to take my cock and my balls and the harness they were gussied-up in like an unbroken bronco. The water on my face was his sweat, the cobweb brush of it his Corona-coloured pubic hair soft as new-washed silk. I clamped down on my tits and I *was* Brad in a frenzy with me pinching him to the moan that was coming out of my chest/his chest.

Oh, this was *gooo-ooood!*

It wasn't long before I thought I couldn't stand Brad's dick in my ass one more second. I pulled him out, stood up shakily, and spewed more cum around that white-on-white tile room than I'd ever shot before, leaning up against the sticky stuff as it rolled down the walls, licking Brad's molasses-thick love juice from the grout as the milk and cream and honey of him ran down the walls toward the floor.

I thought my heart was going to burst through my chest. But I stood there until the hot water was going, going, gone. (I was glad the high-rolling swells up here weren't getting more hot water than we peons were getting down-stairs.)

I turned the nickel-plated, hand-cast taps off and stepped, dripping water, jizz, and lube into the living room. Bodily and man-made fluids seeped into the matte-finished oak, which was, naturally enough, slick underfoot as I walk/slid to the living room's terrace doors and opened them. A blast of air hit me like a plunge into a cold lake. I just stood there, covered in goose flesh, and let it blow me dry.

I watched the sun set over New Jersey and the light come up on the Statue of Liberty's torch until I was brought back from my sex-filled reverie by Atilla sharp-barking down the hall in the distance behind me. Susan and Linda laughed raucously as they carried groceries through the front door of No. 8, slamming the door behind them as if they didn't even *care* who their new next-door neighbour might be.

I let myself out of Brad's place and went home.

I took the bottle with me, of course and wiped fingerprints off doorknobs with my clothes, but I didn't clean up a thing. This was *my* territory and *my*

In The Pitts

mark, I thought. And every time you fuck your new starlet/model girlfriend in your new place, Mr. Pitt, some part of your swollen crimson bite-me lips will be kissing my asshole, and some part of your swollen white-boy dick will be buried to the wheat-field pubes into the wide-open spaces of hospitable me.

Welcome home, honey. How was your day?

DADDY LOVER GOD
by Don Shewey

Sunday is often a busy day, but yesterday was slow. Two sessions, neither of them strictly speaking a massage. It was an afternoon with what I call my client-husbands. There are several of them now among my regulars, men with whom the work has gone beyond erotic massage and into the realm of sacred intimate work, where anything is possible. Sometimes it's a dilemma when more than one of my client-husbands call to book sessions on the same day. They take up a lot of energy, and I prefer to see no more than one a day.

But these two yesterday, Eugene and Lester, were so vastly different that I didn't mind seeing them one right after the other. In fact, it made the afternoon really fun.

Eugene is one of my most intriguing clients. A handsome, rich, and successful African-American book publisher with two kids and a soon-to-be-ex-wife, Eugene turned 44 recently and decided it was time to do some of the things he'd always dreamed about but never done. Being with a man was one of those things. He'd gotten massaged at his health club, but he called me for a private session out of curiosity to see what might happen. I quickly discovered Eugene's pleasure spot was his butt, especially the tender pink skin around his butthole, stroked by a finger or a tongue or the firm head of a hard cock. What really surprised me, though, was how eager Eugene was for hugging and kissing and friendly affectionate interaction. He didn't seem to have a shred of sex-shame or body-shame. I couldn't bring myself to think of him as heterosexual; he was just sexual, period.

Our first few sessions set a pattern. I would stretch him out and massage his back thoroughly, relaxing him and working out the kinks. Eugene was fairly relaxed anyway; he took care of his body and always stopped at his health club to shower and groom himself before a session. I would work my way

Daddy Lover God

down his body to his butt and legs, applying firm pressure when kneading his buttocks, sliding my warm oily hands lightly over his inner thighs (always producing a beautiful cherry-red boner), working on his feet to let the erotic energy subside, then stroking back up the legs to spend time on his butt.

After some stretching, stroking, and rocking, Eugene would be loosened up and ready for further exploration. At first I put on gloves and gave him a full-scale internal prostate massage. But after a few sessions we discussed it and I learned that Eugene preferred the external butt stroking to penetration. What he really liked was for me to lie on top of him, resting the full weight of my body on his back, and tease his butthole with the head of my dick. I would wrap my hands around his pecs and pull him close, nuzzling the back of his neck with my lips and teeth, while he writhed and pushed his butt back against my hips. Sometimes I would get so hot doing this that I would squirt prematurely onto his back, which he never seemed to mind. In fact, he said it turned him on. Inevitably he would roll over and pull me on top of him for some deep tongue-kissing. He would let his huge warm hand slide down my body until it rested over my hairy butt, and we would proceed from there until he was ready to climax. I didn't bother trying to convince Eugene to contain his erotic energy. He was so highly charged, there was no stopping him from coming.

Eugene was full of euphemisms. I enjoyed hearing them and liked to torture them out of him by asking point-blank, "What is the experience you would like to have today?" Eugene was much too polite and respectful to say, "I want you to chow down on my joint" or "Put it up my ass, baby, the way you know I like it." No no no no no. He'd say things like, "Well, I like part one of the massage, and then I'd like to move to part two." Or he'd say, "Depending on how you're feeling, I'd like to have an 'interesting' session rather than a conventional one."

Yesterday, when I asked the question, Eugene dropped the expression "role play." This puzzled me. In the gay world, role-playing generally takes place in SM relationships and the roles are severely defined. Master and slave are the most common, but they can also be as benign as big brother/little brother. Somehow I didn't think that's what Eugene had in mind. Then it dawned on me that for a straight guy accustomed to taking the initiative with women and always dominating, simply to lie back and have someone else take care of you is a role-reversal. What to me seemed like a natural, reciprocal interaction – two guys rolling around together, alternating top and bottom – Eugene considered a psychologically risky abdication of male gender behaviour. Ideal recipe for good sex.

The breakthrough session with Eugene came when I asked him to close his eyes and think for a minute and tell me exactly what experience he wanted. Eugene hesitated and very shyly said, "I want to make love." I rejoiced that he had stated his desire so directly. That night we abandoned the massage table. I pulled down the comforter on my futon, and we spent a lovely hour in bed together. It was the first time Eugene ever had a penis in his mouth. Looking up from between my legs, where he'd been attentively stroking my cock, he murmured, "Can I taste it?" When he got permission, he was trembling. I ran my hand across his wooly hair. "Take your time," I said. "Enjoy it. Really taste my cock. Feel what it feels like in your mouth."

Getting blowjobs from novices isn't the most exciting thing in the world, especially when they get hasty and frenzied and their teeth get in the way. That's why I like to slow them down, to get more tongue, more spit. There's a sort of regression that takes place. Sucking dick is like nursing, and it takes a few minutes to relax and get into it, to go back to the infantile pleasure of sucking for the sake of sucking. For grown men, I notice, infantile feelings often bring up a lot of shame. It feels too good to be that helpless, and that's not permitted. It's a macho thing, too – the man has got to be in control, and one way that shows up in cocksucking is the sucker feels he has to work really hard to make the guy come, so the pleasure of simply sucking gets lost in the mechanical function and the power struggle.

I watched Eugene sucking me with the peaceful detachment of a mother watching her child nurse. "This is what it's like to be a sacred intimate," I thought. "I don't feel the urgent need to come or control the situation. I'm content to be present and let Eugene try on this behaviour. There are harder ways to make a living."

Yesterday we had one of our 'interesting' sessions. Eugene called earlier in the day than usual and arrived for an appointment at noon. After a brief conversation about his latest skiing trip with his children, we undressed each

Daddy Lover God

other and proceeded to sprawl on my bed. The early afternoon sun joined us. In the direct sunlight his skin changed colours. Where I licked his thigh, the wet spot shone yellow against brown. I loved seeing the clear sparkle of pre-cum on the tip of his undying erection in direct sunlight. And the blanket of skylight added a layer of warmth to the crush of our hairy chests together.

"I missed you," Eugene murmured in my ear as he lifted his knees and wrapped them around my waist.

For a fleeting moment I wondered how I really felt about Eugene. I know this will sound funny, but I try not to have personal feelings toward any of my clients. It's specifically because I have no future with any of the men I see that I can bring to them a radical presence. In a way, all my clients are the same man – a combination of Daddy, lover, and God. Sometimes I get lonely after they leave. Sometimes I entertain fantasies that a relationship with a client could expand into something larger and more unpredictable – if not a domestic partnership, then some kind of glamourous or romantic partnership of courtesan and patron, with free trips to exotic destinations. But I know I can only get hurt if I expect anything from them. The last time Eugene had visited, he was on his way to a blind date with a famous black opera diva. When he didn't call for three weeks, after a pattern of coming to see me every week, I assumed that Eugene had clicked with the diva and decided to terminate his exploration of mansex.

So my heart lifted and opened at Eugene's tender confession.

"I missed you, too," I said.

In some ways this is the best kind of lovemaking on earth. Both of us set aside time to be together, devoting ourselves to pleasure and connection. All the sex manuals and marriage counsellors advise couples to set aside time for lovemaking, but how many people actually do that? In my experience, scheduling lovemaking usually creates anxiety and resentment and imitations of arousal. In the context of a sacred intimate session, both parties rise to the occasion. Of course, there is a financial transaction – the client wants to get his money's worth, and the professional wants to earn his keep. Marxists might call this the commodification of desire, and Puritans might frown on the sale of what should properly be given freely. Sometimes I feel cynical about the work and observe myself going through the motions. I'm performing work-for-hire masquerading as unconditional love. I'm peddling counterfeit romance to men too deprived or depraved to complain. Those are the accusations I fling at myself.

But in the best of times, the work feels not like consumer carnality but focused ritual. Ritual in the sense of creating time out of time with a specific intention. We are here not to talk about the weather or the stock market, or to run power trips on each other, but to do something we don't get very many opportunities to do – open our hearts and bodies to someone else.

I must have been getting a little corny and overly spiritual in my reverie, because Eugene suddenly raised his head and looked me in the eye. "When are we going to go all the way?" he asked. Then I remembered that I really was dealing with a straight man, whose experience of sex centres on intercourse-to-ejaculation, in contrast to which everything else is hors d'oeurves.

"Going all the way" with Eugene tempts me. If there is any scenario that justifies fucking without rubbers, here's a pretty good one – a "straight" guy who's never been fucked, a wealthy businessman with no drug habits. I'm as certain as I can be that I'm HIV-negative. What would be the harm of going in bareback? He'd love it. I'd love it. Skip that awkward moment of freezing the pelvis while struggling with the condom pack (not easy to rip open with lube-smeared fingers), trying to stay hard while putting the rubber on, inevitably putting it on upside down to begin with, reservoir tip UP so the rest of it rolls DOWN the shaft, and then aiming for the hole and hoping it yields immediately so the friction of sliding in and out can rejuvenate any diminishment of erection...

I wondered what Eugene did with the women he slept with. Did he use rubbers? Did they insist? Eugene clearly has no trouble staying hard. He's usually hard the entire time he spends with me.

The angel choir of Safe Sex Precautions and Professional Integrity danced in my head, with some semi-legal language about the "slippery slope." I have a responsibility! To educate guys who are out of the safe sex loop, exactly like Eugene! At the moment, I didn't feel like educating. So I avoided the whole question by positioning myself so he could feel my cock pulsing against his butthole, and I rocked my hips against the back of his butt and thighs, for that all-important first chakra awakening sensation. For me,

Daddy Lover God

hardly anything feels better than butthole-surfing. Still, I knew Eugene craved the sensation of penetration, if only out of curiosity.

Maybe it would happen another day.

When we were done, Eugene dressed slowly, chatting all the way. I didn't want to rush him, but as soon as the door closed, I had to rush around like a madman. I didn't have to put fresh sheets on the table, because we'd skipped that part. But I saged the room, hopped in the shower, closed the curtains, and then changed clothes. Out of my sweat pants and T-shirt, into my leather pants, white tank-top, leather vest, and high-top Timberland boots: an outfit that predictably brought a sigh of pleasure from Lester when he came in the door.

Lester looks more like Humpty Dumpty than anyone I've ever met. A middle manager in his late 50s, he recently shaved his mustache and cut his white hair short, so his large head looks paler and more egg-like than ever. Over six feet tall, he probably weighs 250 pounds, including a big soft white underexercised belly.

He walked in the door and handed me a black plastic shopping bag. Inside was a white plastic shopping bag with the handles tied in a knot. In addition to his usual wrist and ankle restraints, he brought some new toys that he'd picked up cheap from a one-man bazaar at the Eagle: a black leather dog collar and a black Spandex hood with a single mouth-hole for breathing.

"Have you tried them out?" I asked.

"Yes," he said.

"How do they feel?"

"They feel great. I can see through the hood, though."

I instructed him to remove his black turtleneck, and I fastened the dog collar around his neck. I pulled the hood over his head and then went to my bureau drawer to get a foam-padded blackout blindfold and strapped that over the hood. I restrained his wrists behind his back, noticing drops of anxious sweat already trickling along his flabby sides. Unfastening his belt, I roughly yanked his denim pants to his knees and smacked his ankles until he spread his feet wide. Then I tugged his white cotton underpants down as well, freeing a big fat smooth-headed boner (already drooling pre-cum) and giant balls. I walked across the room to fetch a length of clothesline from a drawer, and when I turned back I stopped for a minute to take in the sight in front of me: a giant schlumpy black-hooded Igor with a deserted lot of scraggly graying hair on his droopy chest standing with his pants around his knees, sporting an erection, wearing a dog collar with his hands tied behind his back, and gulping shallow breaths through his goldfish mouth. This is truly sacred work, I thought.

I stood in front of him and tied the clothesline to the largest ring on his dog collar. I let the other end of the clothesline fall to the floor and then wrapped it around his cock and balls several times, which made his dick bob toward the ceiling higher and harder. Now a long line of liquid dripped from the tip of his dick down to the carpet. (Good thing I'm not very Suzy Homemaker, hysterical about spills and stains.) I grabbed the rope at chest level and plucked it gently, tugging his neck and balls at the same time. I let myself enjoy playing with Lester in this state. No rush.

I knelt at his feet and one after the other lifted his legs and removed his trousers. Then I walked behind him and, sliding a hand down one arm after the other, I unsnapped the wrist restraints. Walking in front of him again, I unwrapped the clothesline from around his balls and said, "I want you to get down on your knees."

As he lurched forward, I added, "Slowly!"

Grunting, he dropped first to one knee, then the other.

"Okay, now get down on all fours." I adjusted the dog collar so the ring the line was attached to slid around to the back of his neck. "We're going to go for a little walk."

I led him across the room, steering him with slight tugs on the rope. When I got to the hallway, I didn't say anything but let him find his bearings between the radiator (going full blast) and the wall. Leading him down the hall, I realised we would be passing the window in the hallway and wondered if anyone in the adjacent apartments happened to be standing at their windows looking this way. If so, they were getting the kind of show urban voyeurs long for and rarely find.

I herded Lester into my small bathroom. I pushed the toilet cover up against the tank with a loud ceramic crack. Then I pushed the toilet seat up

Daddy Lover God

so it also made a distinct sound.

"Are you thirsty?" I asked the figure on the floor.

"No, sir," came the faint reply.

"Are you sure?"

"Yes, sir."

After a few rounds of boot-kissing and sitting-up-and-begging, I walked him back to the living room and had him kneel on a pillow on the floor while I attached the wrist restraints to the end of the massage table. I took my wide leather belt off and gave Lester the strapping that he eagerly anticipated at every session. This turned out to be a good position. Usually I tie him down to the table on his belly. On his knees, he could stick his butt way out – a sign of pleasure and a request for more – and lengthen his back for the strokes on the upper back and shoulders that he seemed to like even more than lashes across his expansive white butt. I also noticed the strapping made him rock hard, a fact that lying on the table usually concealed.

Finished with that, I had him crawl up onto the table and lie on his back, still blindfolded, hooded, and manacled. I opened a bureau drawer and took out my braided nylon bondage ropes. I secured his feet to the end of the massage table and pulled his arms up over his head. Then I wound the longest rope I had around his mountainous belly and under the table and tied it up tight. Then I brought his arms down and secured them to the ropes. I got out a set of Walkman headphones, plugged them into the stereo system, positioned them over Lester's ears, and turned on some spacy and vaguely sinister electronic music quite loud. His shiny red apple of a dickhead pointed straight up to the ceiling.

I stood back and examined my work and saw that it was good.

My experience in tying people up is laughably limited. Lester would have been surprised to know that he was my only SM client. He repeatedly marvelled at my ingenuity and expertise at taking him on journeys through intense body play. If the truth be known, I surprise myself almost every time I see Lester. Although the practice of massaging someone centres on being radically present and paying attention to the individual body on the table in front of you, most of my massage sessions follow the same routine, touching the same spots in the same order each time. Even lovemaking sessions with my favourite sex partners tend to follow the same pattern after a while, once we've worked out what we like. These sessions with Lester, though, permit and even require much more spontaneity than I'm used to.

It actually terrifies me. I hate having to be spontaneous. I much prefer having a script in front of me, a road map. But more and more I find myself having fun in these sessions with Lester. Working with someone who is blindfolded, restrained (no touching back), and often sound-sealed, I can operate without being seen. Sometimes I feel like a scientist working in a laboratory, mixing this chemical with that chemical and observing which makes the liquid turn green and which produces clouds of vapour. There is a lot of Frankenstein involved, too – I measure the effect of my actions by how much the creature on the table twitches and jerks.

I often find myself thinking, as I'm feeding Lester a ripe strawberry or a teaspoon of his own copious pre-cum, or as I'm stroking his engorged penis with the blossom of a rose, This is as intimate as I've ever been with anybody. I've never done this even with a lover.

I had about 15 minutes left to play with Lester in this state. I rummaged around in my basket of playthings and pulled out a handful of clothespins. I fastened one to his right nipple, which made him jump, and then another to the left. He rocked slightly from side to side, and his fleshpole danced with pleasure. In quick succession I attached three clothespins to his scrotum, starting at the bottom near his perineum up to the base of his shaft, the wooden clips forming a kind of peacock's fan spreading out over the top of his balls, which were as big as a juice orange. Very aesthetically pleasing.

After a pause, I stuck a few more clothespins on some other sensitive areas: the sides of his belly, just below his armpits, his inner thighs. Then I hung back and let the endorphins kick in. I knew that, far from being tortured, Lester was having a ball. Not only was he feeling sensations in parts of his gargantuan body that usually spent their days numb and dead, he was also being closely attended by a hot studly leatherman. It was like having a Broadway show performed just for you.

I reached over and fiddled with the stereo system, hiking the volume up and fucking with the fast-forward button so the music sped up and slowed down.

Daddy Lover God

It was getting to be time to stop. I quickly pulled the clothespins off of Lester's body in reverse order. At each removal, a shudder would ripple through his system. When I got to the nipples, I squeezed each clothespin harder until I got a whimper of response, and then unfastened it. I walked into the kitchen and plucked a pink plastic-handled feather-duster off a hook. I took it to the massage table and lightly brushed each of the spots where a clothespin had been. I lingered at Lester's balls. Brushing up and down the scrotum, barely touching them with the feathers, made his slightly drooping dick harder and redder. I returned the feather-duster to its hook and began untying the ropes. I took my time, coiling each rope and knotting it for storage before going on to the next. Cleaning up while I go saves me time later, and it gives Lester a few more minutes to stay in his trance. I could tell that he had gone pretty deep this time, because his body was very relaxed and his breathing was quiet.

Once the ropes and restraints were removed, I had him sit up on the table. "I'm going to count backwards from five to zero, and when I get to zero, we'll be done." As I counted down, I kneaded his shoulders and unhooked his dog collar. I slid the blindfold off, and as I got to "Zero," I pulled off the hood.

He looked up at me with the docile, shining eyes of a newborn chick. A puddle of gratitude and satisfaction, he seemed more like a five-year-old child than a middle-aged man.

"Sometime," he said, "you're going to have to figure out what your overnight rate would be."

Lester almost always makes a comment like that when the scene is over: he wants it to go on and on. He once even proposed marriage, pointing out the excellent health benefits his company offered the spouse equivalents of employees. I take these comments as compliments to my work, but they also make me a little nervous. I guess I recognise in Lester my own aggressive instinct to concretize my desires. Sometimes, though, fantasies are more potent when they remain in the fantasy realm. That's why I've never taken off my clothes in front of him and never given him a 'release.' I want him to consider me a guide along the journey of coming out (as a gay man and as an SM practitioner), not the destination.

When he made his half-joking request for an overnight session, I felt a little badly, because I knew that as much as Lester enjoys the SM play, he really wants to be held and loved. What are the chances of a fat bald middle-aged man who's just come out of the closet finding a lover? It's not impossible, but it takes as much inner work as getting out there and hunting. I wanted to give Lester a pep talk about self-esteem, to urge him to look inside himself for validation rather than outside. But that seemed tricky coming out of a session that revolved around wearing a dog collar and having clothespins fastened to his nipples.

I recently flipped through a paperback book of SM fantasies called Sir, looking for new ideas of what to do with Lester. I was getting a little tired of the routine we'd established – dog training, strapping, bondage. I read through the stories. They weren't very interesting. Most of them involved teenage or college-age boys having their first experiences with a man. None of them involved a fat middle-aged bald man seeking experience in the hands of a professional masseur.

I tried to remember what I'd been like as a kid, full of yearning for experience. When every physical encounter felt like a judgment from heaven on my worth as a person. In high school I knew for certain I was queer. I was in love with two of my friends: tall and talkative Lenny Meltzer, whose mother was the art teacher at school, and dark, handsome Ron Garrett, whose father was a general and who wanted to be a priest. I would go for long walks in the woods with Lenny, talking about the pseudo-philosophical stuff young intellectuals discuss, while fantasising ripping off his shirt and holding him to my heart. Ron and I would sit in his family car late at night after play rehearsals, talking for an hour when, to my mind, we could have been making out.

My fantasies about Lenny and Ron were less sexual than romantic. It was the jocks at school who stirred up my beastly fantasies. Listening to them brag about the number of times they'd fucked girls, I conceived hot scenarios in which I'd be alone in the locker room when tall, long-legged football star Jack Mundy would wander in from his shower with half a boner and sit on the bench drying his crotch over and over again, looking at me with an attitude of pugnacious challenge mixed with a vulnerable curiosity...

I was 19 before I ever had a dick in my mouth, and I felt like I was years behind then. Imagine being 57 and never having sucked a cock. "Why bother coming out?" Lester complained, and I had a hard time arguing with him on that point.

When I began my massage practice, I unthinkingly assumed that everyone in the world had the same images and associations with being gay that I have. For me, coming out as a college student during the mid-1970s in politically active Boston meant entering a community, gaining self-knowledge, finding a place in the world, and enjoying almost limitless sexual opportunities. Seeing so many clients who are married, closeted, or coming out late in life, I've come to realise that their associations with being gay are much more negative and frightening. Embracing a gay identity for them means jettisoning another that, for better or worse, has served them for a lifetime. Being gay is just as likely to conjure a sense of loss and shrinking horizons as to spell freedom and expansion. And for many of them, sexual satisfaction will only occur through encounters with professionals. Admitting these realities makes me sad and angry, and it increases my compassion for older guys who didn't have the same chances I had – a compassion I'm not always able to show. It does make me wonder what my life will be like when I'm 60. I assume that I will be partnered and sexually satisfied, but for all I know I'll be just like Lester, investing my emotions in unrequited affairs with young erotic masseurs.

After Lester left, I decided to give myself a sacred intimate session. I turned off all the electric lights in the apartment, leaving the candles flickering on the mantelpiece and on the ancestors' altar. I put on my favourite ambient music, a spacy disk with unpredictable eruptions of bass-heavy sex-groove riffs. I peeled off my Tom Petty and the Heartbreakers T-shirt and my black drawstring sweat pants. And I gathered supplies. One bottle of coconut oil was still warm from the last session. I dug around in the middle drawer of my supply bureau and brought out my personal-use dildo, which was slightly smaller, more friendly, more human than the somewhat imposing dildo I used with clients. Grabbing a tube of K-Y, I climbed aboard the massage table, still slightly cool and damp with oil.

I lay on my back and slid the cushioned face plate under the middle of my back, which pushed my chest out while my shoulders relaxed backwards. I took deep breaths. For all my coaching of clients, I knew I didn't breathe as much as I could either. Breathing brings up all kinds of feelings and sensations. It opens you up to the possibility of pleasure, but it also makes you acutely aware of aches and pains in your body as well as whatever emotions you've been avoiding all day. I registered the dull ache that usually shows up in my lower back on the right side at the end of a day. I felt the heaviness in my balls and wondered if it was related to my lower back pain. Kidneys? Backed-up jizz? I hadn't come for two weeks and had experienced raging hard-ons practically every day. Sure, some Chinese practitioners could go for ten years without coming. But I felt quite certain that my own body was getting a little fried with frustration. I am my own cocktease, I thought. My cock had been gearing up to shoot every day now, all the neurons and pistons and hydraulics on alert and ready to spring into action. I had a moment of understanding why the United States was always getting drawn into conflagrations abroad. If you spend half the national budget on defense, employing a million hot-blooded American males to be ready to fight, they're going to get very antsy if they don't get to blow off some steam every now and then. Hey, maybe I should write a grant application to the Pentagon, proposing a giant annual orgy, a week-long sexual Olympics, in lieu of invading some tiny foreign country populated by non-white people. This would primarily be aimed at servicemen between the ages of 18 and 25. There would be physique competitions, how-many-times-can-you-come contests, how-far-can-you-shoot matches, circle jerks, blowjob booths. I would personally volunteer to supervise the festivities. Yes, I would write that proposal.

Later, though. Right now I was oiling up my half-hard cock and thinking about Jacob. He was one of the few clients I had crossed the cocksucking barrier with. It was an extraordinary experience to play with Jacob. I always gave him a good thorough massage. He was relaxed, tan (maintained by frequent trips to South Beach and the local tanning salon), and well-groomed. He trimmed his body hair closely. I prefer untrimmed body hair, but the way Jacob attends to his seems to have no purpose other than erotic. I'm pleased to inspect the careful way he shaves his balls and razors his pubic hair up to the top of his beautiful fat dick, which begins to swell as soon as I lay my hands on his body.

The routine is that I don't introduce any erotic touch for the first hour, until

Daddy Lover God

Jacob has gotten stretched and pummelled and all the kinks worked out of his back. Then when I roll him over onto his back again, I lightly stroke the tips of his close-cropped body hair, from his clavicle to his big toes and back. After stroking the full length of his body, I do another length with one hand while using the other to lightly brush his nipples, which I know sends him through the roof. Before long, his cock is rock-hard and pointing at his chin. I stand at his head and brush both nipples while breathing quietly into his ear, encouraging him to fill his body with oxygen, to feel the erotic energy all over his body. He has a tendency to catch his breath, hold it for a while, take in a little bit at a time. I have to keep reminding him to breathe all the way down to his toes.

I lean across his face to stroke his chest and his belly. The curly hair on my chest and torso tickles his nose, and he begins to nudge my body, keeping his eyes closed, like a newborn puppy blindly finding its way to sustenance. I climb onto the table, carefully kneeling on either side of his head, and proceed to plant a line of very, very soft kisses down his belly, to his shaved balls, and eventually to the dripping, bouncing head of his dick. Opening wide, I invite his cock into the warm wetness of my mouth. After a couple of preliminary strokes, I take him all the way into my throat, like a key going into a lock. And I rest there, lying flat on top of Jacob, our warm hairy bellies smushed together, and I breathe through my nose, while he moans softly, his cock twitching, the full length of it buried in my mouth. I've almost never experienced this ecstasy before. It's a cocksucker's dream: the Perfect Fit.

I replayed this scene, lying back on a maroon bedsheet, my oily cock in one hand. It didn't take much to get fully stiff, thinking about Jacob. If only he were here right now. If only he and I could permit ourselves to indulge in an hour-long blowjob, rather than a few minutes snatched at the end of a massage session. I felt down between my legs and ran a fingertip around the bulging pucker of my asshole. I snapped open the fliptop tube of K-Y and squeezed a drop onto my forefinger, and then smeared it over my butthole and easily slid the finger in up to the first knuckle. It wasn't so often that I played with my own butt, so I decided to go all the way.

I got up on my knees and faced the mirror over the fireplace. I extracted another gob of lubricant from the long white tube and slathered it on the head and shaft of my rubber husband. Then I positioned the dildo at the opening to my butt. It immediately slid in just past the head. I stopped and took a breath. My cock had wilted a little bit during these maneuvers, so I stroked myself again. My hands were gooey from the K-Y. I wiped one hand on the sheet and returned it to my cock. With the other hand I pinched first one nipple, then the other. Concentrating on my breathing, I opened my ass to receive more of the dildo. Suddenly, a rush of heat spread all over my body, down my legs, through my hips and butt, up my spine to the back of my neck. I slowed down my cock strokes, then sped them up. I was so close. I loved this fullness. I thought of all the cocks I'd loved sitting on, and the ones I'd fantasised sitting on, filling me up and rocking and rocking and holding and pushing and heat hot full hot gasp stop stop can't stop oh oh oh oh. I spilled a torrent of thick white juice onto the blood-red sheet. It looked like a map of all the Great Lakes: Lake Michigan, Lake Huron, Lake Ontario, Lake Erie, Lake Superior.

FULL SERVICE
by David Evans

Billy realised as he and Adam drove up to the carwash that he had indeed stayed longer at Adam's scaffolding business than he had intended. It was now the end of October, still very warm for London although the lure of the winter sun and the dry heat of the sand dunes of Las Palmas and the Gran Canaria was beginning to appear pretty potent. But there was another, equally irresistible force holding Billy back.

Although he hadn't fallen in love as he thought he easily might, Billy Stiles had fallen deeply in lust. Since the first night when Adam Plummer had dropped his sweats as he stood in the first floor window of that old house in the Caledonian Road looking down on Billy in the scaffolders yard below, Billy had been unable to resist the constant, almost magnetic lure of the thought of Adam's cock waiting kitted up inside the tight sport shorts Adam wore for modesty's sake beneath his dirty scaffolder's sweat pants. Anything looser would have advertised, and during the working day, Adam felt more comfortable with his donkey dick firmly disguised.

Indelibly imprinted on Billy's mind was that first memory of seeing Adam's thumbs hitch down the front of his sweats and then hooking up the tight leg of the Adidas shorts out of which sprang a cock the size of which Billy was sure he had never believed existed. Even from one floor down and twenty feet away, Billy could see the seam of the huge main vein winding like a purple river beneath the firm fleshy surface of the shaft, pumping that throughput of fullness, feeding the cock's head, engorging it so that all on its own, the sculptured helmet forced Adam's foreskin back, rolling it away like the canvas on a Wimbledon centre court.

Billy had stood transfixed to the spot, unable to move, his mouth dropped open, his jaw hanging slackly like he was in a trance. He managed to summon up the presence of mind to look behind him, wondering for a moment with only a vague sense of concern how much the people in the houses bordering the yard might see, but there was only the blank wall of the side of a pub. Billy dropped to one knee in the yard, felt his own dick harden, and twitched his sphincter a couple of times to make sure it was still active. Billy always got horny for a second shag and his impetus was already in full tilt. It hadn't been an hour since his hole had been stretched by Jim, the foreman whose rough hands had tested Billy's asshole roughly before shagging him quickly, too rushed, with a full hard nine inches pounding crudely deep into Billy as the astonished tenant of the third floor apartment looked on at the fantasy scene on the scaffolding outside his very bedroom window.

But that had been all of an hour ago. It took much less than an hour for Billy's rampant, insatiable libido to charge up again. He was quite ready when Adam beckoned Billy up with a little come-on gesture of both hands, shifting his position as he did so that he stood with his legs apart, the full span of his cock pressed against the cold window glass. It looked like the biggest uncut sausage in butcher's cling film.

"Oh, boy!" Billy whistled as his legs just-managed to carry him as he ran from the yard up to the first floor backroom Adam used as an office.

Upstairs, when he got there, he saw to his relief that Adam had put his cock back into his shorts. Billy wanted to relive that moment again and again, that moment when the dick of dicks, the king of cocks fell out of those white shorts and slapped against Adam's hairy thigh. One of those moments, Billy thought, like when he'd seen the whale's huge tail slap the surface of the water in the Catalina channel off LA. Unforgettable.

Adam was taller, much taller than Billy, bigger too, like the slower following whale to Billy's leading, dancing dolphin. Adam had held Billy close to him for a long time, grinding his hips into Billy's flesh as though he was a drill-engine sinking a well, searching out the crevices, the lines of least resistance.

For longer than usual, Billy had held out. Billy wanted to be kissed at that moment more than he wanted to sink to his knees and watch the whale dive .. It was a moment somewhat alien to the young Londoner who

Full Service

was usually down on a cock faster than a plumber's plunger onto a blocked drain but, although he wanted to be romanced by this big bear of a man, when he realised that no kiss was forthcoming, it didn't spoil Billy's pleasure in the slightest. Like no way.

But it changed his perspective. He knew that the score between him and this wonderful man was going to be down to a one day match, in cricketing parlance, rather than the sustained strategy of a test series. But, hey... Nothing wrong with that. Far from it. Billy merely set aside romance as he abandoned himself to the sheer carnality of the moment, letting his body slide through Adam's enveloping embrace and slipping down over Adam's strongly-defined chest, squeezing over the washboard abs and allowing his own chest to be the first part of him to take the impression of the swollen, straining barrel of fuck artillery which Adam was fielding.

The shorts came undone with three little buttons down one side. Billy had made this process of releasing Adam's cock last as long as he could, only popping the third, lowest button when he'd licked Adam's shorts wetter than a tea towel at Christmas.

"Go on, Billy," Adam murmured again and again as Billy's tongue and playful nibbles excited the man almost to the point of pain. Billy loved to use his teeth, gently nipping at the roll of skin which had been furled like a spinnaker around the circumference of Adam's dickhead. "Eat my cock, for chrissake. Go on. Get on it."

"Urrgghh!" Billy agreed as he slurped yet more lubricating saliva over the straining fabric of the shorts, pulling them tight over the huge landscape of knob that throbbed and twitched as his tongue found the tiny g-spots just behind the head where the pulled-back skin is taut, where the head becomes the shaft ...

"Fuckin' too right, man!"

Billy pulled back from his wet work to see the moment he'd delayed so tantalisingly.

His finger and thumb eased the third and final button almost out of the buttonhole. He looked up to see Adam looking down at him, a look of such pleading in his eyes.

David Evans

"I always wanna remember the first time I saw your dick, man," Billy said, placing Adam's hands on the gold, specially made tit-rings which hung from his sore nipples. "You got summat to do, an' all. Get yourself to work on my tits, yeah?"

As Adam squeezed with both thumbs and forefingers, pressing Billy's pink/brown nip-nubs hard against the heavy gold sleepers, Billy cried out and at the same time popped the button. Adam had of course seen his dick every day for all his life; he should have been quite used to it, but that night, in his office lit only by its bare lightbulb and stacked with untidy piles of dusty old materials catalogues, empty paint tins and junk-covered desk, Adam seemed to be seeing his dick for the first time, almost in slow motion as the foot long thing fell down against his leg like a giant leafless treetrunk felled by a lumberjack to the forest floor. Shit, Adam thought, it really is big.

And it was still getting harder, taking its own sweet time just like those great cocks always seem to do. Like they're meant to do.

Yeah, they never seem hard, Billy remembered thinking as he gauged size, length, girth and translated these three assessed statistics into how wide and how deep he opened his throat. Let me fuckin' at it, please!

Adam had no chance on that occasion to see how his cock aroused, inflamed, and drove crazy the guy kneeling at his feet for Billy had fallen onto it instinctively and after re-positioning it inside his mouth a couple of times, getting the hang of the thing, went down on the whole pillar, sinking the whole great baby's arm of a dick deep into his throat.

"Orrrgghh!" Adam gasped. He'd never been taken like that, not so immediately and so easily. He looked down and saw the back of Billy's cropped blonded head pumping slowly up and down onto his crotch like a backyard oil well in Bakersfield, allowing Adam to gain greatest pleasure from the fabulous fellatio the younger man was performing.

Just Adam's maximum pleasure? Oh, puhleeze! Billy knew from how much his eyes watered and from how he reacted to Adam's fingers kneading his nipples into ecstasy that this was the best sex he'd ever had. And it hadn't even started yet, because Billy knew when a man was a comer and when he was a stayer. Adam was a stayer. After a while, Billy

Full Service

rose from his knees and perched on the corner of Adam's desk. Adam leant forward and with both his arms swept the desk clear of papers and dross and then with the fingers of his right hand fluttering against Billy's asshole, he slowly pushed Billy back until the younger man was resting on his elbows, spread-eagled on the desktop.

"I'm gonna fuck you, Billy," Adam whispered, pulling off Billy's boots as Billy raised his legs in the air, exposing the still moist hole which Jim the foreman had only an hour ago just finished shagging. He tossed Billy's boots into a corner and then pulled off Billy's own sweats and his day-old cK jockstrap. Billy brought his legs to rest, heels on the edge of the desk. "I've bin thinkin' about doin' this all the damn day long not to mention most of last night."

"Worth the wait?" Billy asked, smiling mysteriously. Adam had produced a tube of lube and squeezed a whole load out onto his chest.

"You bet," Adam replied as he threw the tube away and dipped his fingers into the gooey gel, inserting first one and then the others, one after the other and then all together into Billy's smooth ass. "You ready for this fucker?" he murmured, nodding down to where his cucumber-dimensioned tool glistened bright and hard, still wet with Billy's spit.

"When it's dressed up," Billy said, fixing Adam's eyes with a concentrated stare. He wanted to see the rubber rolling down over that knob. He wanted to fix the moment in his mind for when the lean times came. Lean times? For Billy Stiles? Like never.

Then Adam lost his nerve. In truth, he hadn't fucked anyone for a long, long time. He'd ripped the packet, pulled the rubber out. His dick was resting against Billy's hole and Billy had spread his legs as far apart as he could and was bent over, almost double, anxious not to miss the moment. He wanted to watch the invasion of his ass real bad, like it was the biggest big match ever.

"You're never gonna take this," Adam said quickly, shocked by how huge his cock looked against Billy's sun-tanned thighs, how impossibly big the head looked as it locked against the smooth skin of Billy's shaved asshole which had already inexplicably started to ooze. "I can't ..."

"'Course you can. You worry about yourself. Let me worry about me.

I'm jus' fine, so dress the fucker up and stick it to me, man." Billy breathed heavily, earnestly. He knew he was wet. Wondered if it was ... but he knew it was just his special lube. Natural lube that just seemed to arrive.

Billy gasped as he watched Adam roll on the extra large rubber, couldn't believe that the latex fabric didn't rip apart as it slowly covered the length of the heavy shaft. For one moment, even Billy wondered ...

"Okay," Adam said breathing deeply too. "How d'you wanna do this, Billy."

Billy grinned.

"I'm not made of porcelain," he replied. "Just poke it into me." He wriggled pressing down a little as he felt the head of Adam's cock engage with his sphincter. This was consummate. This was ultimate as far as Billy was concerned. His lips parted and his eyes flared open as he held Adam's gaze with his own just as the enormous cockhead parted the lips of his sphincter and disappeared. Adam stopped, almost pulled back but Billy leant forward and grabbed his guy by the cheeks of his ass and stopped him withdrawing. "No!" he insisted. "You gotta fuck me, man. Please. I'm fine ..." Billy wondered if Adam might kiss him then but ... He needn't have worried. Adam was not about to settle down.

What he was about to do was shag into Billy like a train chugging into a long hill tunnel. Adam couldn't believe how easily Billy took his dick.

"You're in, guy," Billy acknowledged, smiling with deepest contentment and fulfilment as he felt the onward motion of deeper penetration of his bowels stop for there was nowhere else for Adam to go. Adam was in up to the hilt of his very being. "Now you're gonna fuck me really properly, right?"

And so Adam started. He found himself convinced by Billy's own confidence and started to pump. Billy threw his legs everywhere. He yelled at times, the effort to keep going was so great. The desk was on casters and it moved around the lino of the small office with each thrust that Adam's hips made. Billy laughed and whooped as this ride-of-a-lifetime took him to the heights of pleasure. He even found himself crying at one stage, sobbing and panting as Adam's cock rammed repeatedly into his prostate, almost hurting him with the most sublime sexual orchestration.

Full Service

He wanted to come, suddenly became terrified of coming and spoiling everything, but he managed in the nick of time to shift his position on the desktop so that the rampaging cockhead, like a frantic caged beast, found different, more neutral tissue to farrow against.

"I think I'm gonna come, Billy," Adam announced through clenched teeth. Billy and the desk were now rammed against the office door. "You ready for it?"

"Ready or not ... It's now or never, Adam!" Billy cried as he felt the acceleration in Adam's hip-plunging thrusts and the pressure of Adam's handplay on his nipples increase to being almost unbearable. "Do it to me! Do it FOR me!!"

"Aaaaggghhh!" Adam yelled as he thrust for the last time into Billy's ass before withdrawing and expertly whipping off the rubber and shooting a spurting fountain of goopy jism over Billy's heaving, breathless chest, massaging the spunk after each ejaculation into Billy's body with his huge, spatulate hands. "Oh Billy! Billeee!" he groaned as he sank exhausted over Billy's equally exhausted frame and hugged onto it as though it was the last life-raft in lost space.

How long they'd held onto each other that night. It should have gone on, Billy thought as he gently accelerated Adam's car into the entrance to the carwash. It should've but it didn't ...

Not that Billy was unhappy. Not that he was bored. It was just that he knew he should now be moving on but ... But how?

The young man who came to the car window asked Adam what he wanted: standard, complete, or a full service. Did he grin just a little bit too broadly? As he bent down, the guy proved to be someone Billy immediately recognised. He hadn't seen Jimmy Chappell since school, but they had grown up together in the neighbourhood and they'd both known, though never acknowledged, that the other was gay. Seen each other in the local cottages when they were learning. There are some things gay guys just know.

"That you, Jimmy?" Billy called out. Jimmy, about the same size and weight as Billy, ducked down and took a peek at the driver of this car. The passenger he'd already noticed. He'd seen Adam around. Even thought that he might just be ... Possibly be ... There are some things gay guys just know.

"Hey, Billy Stiles? How are you? I thought you was in Ibiza?"

"Came back din' I? Needed to see me auntie and to earn a bit more to take me out there again."

"You goin' back, then?" Jimmy asked. "Not good enough for you, are we?"

In a split second, Billy clocked the look on Jimmy' Chappell's face as he glanced across at Adam who was sitting stretched out in the passenger seat, his white Levis turning his long muscular legs into two pillars of carved erotic rock supporting... Billy glanced up at Adam, who seemed equally happy to feast his eyes on Jimmy. Adam's legs were pillars supporting the obvious pediment of a growing hard-on. At night, Adam wanted to advertise. Tonight he looked like a sexgod, a fantasyman. Jimmy Chappell was no slouch in the looks department either and even in his loose sweats, his body displayed Billy's same easy, loping action. A body that could bend, supple ... legs that could be put anywhere, legs that could get round anything.

"Yeah," Billy nodded, "probably next week. Got enough together now to last me the winter. Life's better in the sun, in'it?"

"Oh, I dunno," Jimmy replied, leaning on the window sill of the passenger door, his ass jutting out at rightangles. Jimmy wanted to see better what it was that he could hardly believe in Adam's jeans. "I think the Cally's as good a place as any. Not that I don't like holidays. I went to the Caribbean earlier this year. Loved it an' all that but it's good to come home, innit?"

He paused, grinning full-on at Adam, remembering how the guys on the clipper who had fucked him every night for two weeks looked not unlike Billy Stiles' mate. Jimmy was in top gear, full come-on, sensing that between Billy and Adam there were no complications, no ties that bound. "I like home ground, me. Know what I mean?" Jimmy added, like he wanted to be introduced. To Adam. Not to Billy.

Billy knew. Two little entrepreneurs from the borough getting together? What could be better?

Full Service

"I'm Adam," said Adam, stretching his left hand through the window which Billy shook and held for a little moment longer than necessary. "Adam Plummer. I think I'll get out while Billy drives the motor through the wash, eh? You need to be paid, I s'pose, don't you?" He winked. Billy saw Adam wink. "Is that okay, to get out of the car?"

"Course," Jimmy replied, "you can come and wait in the office. As you can see we're not busy. In fact you're the last through. In fact, to show you how special you are, last customers an' all, I'll just shut the doors up. You can 'ave the full service all to yourself, okay?" Jimmy reached behind him, pressed a button on the wall and the rolldown metal doors of the car wash whirred and clanked down their sashes, closing off the entrance. At the same time, the doors at the exit end also closed.

"Take it on, Billy," Adam said, coolly, with a broad grin. "See you at the other end, huh?"

"You will," Billy grinned and put up the window, sealing the car off once again. Yeah, he thought to himself as he reflected on Adam's total lack of surprise when he announced that he would be off abroad the following week ... Yeah, he concluded, Adam had obviously thought from the start that Billy was too rare a bird to even attempt to cage. Billy smiled. Yeah, he told himself, probably right an' all.

In front of him, the two carwash guys stood in their gear, waiting for him, their nozzled jet-sprays at the ready. There was a black guy and a white, both big, both pretty good-looking except the African looked a bit scary with scars on his cheeks. But both, Billy knew instinctively, had incredible bodies. The white guy slipped off the top half of his green wet-protecs, showing a musculature which had been worked on with the deepest affection. He beckoned Billy to drive forward. Both men, Billy noticed, stared at him intently. They shared a conspiratorial grin, both of them pointing in the direction of Jimmy's office. Jimmy peeked quickly in the rearview mirror to see Adam and Jimmy disappearing into the tinted glass office. Billy looked forward again, caught the mood and grinned. Then it was the black guy's turn to peel off his coverall.

As soon as Billy had stopped the car, engine still running, in position, they came forward, one on either side of the car and began jet-cleaning the wheels and the arches. Both kept looking at Billy inside the car as a fine spray of water misted up the glass. Then one leaned against the window, jetting the hard ray of water onto the roof of the car. It drummed, ominously. Not threatening, just exciting ... The other washguy did the same and Billy looked right, then left ...

As the carwashers stood back to assess their progress, Billy looked at the white guy closer and, unmistakably, saw that he was wearing no underwear beneath the thin green nylon, soaked through at the end of a long, busy shift. He turned quickly and checked out the African. Same story, man. Not a shred of any underthreads what-so-fuckin'-ever.

Jeez! The thought flashed across his mind as the two men went back to their work ... Both were pressing their wet nylon-covered hips against the window glass. Both almost immediately had growing hard-ons. What the fuck to do?

Billy, unseen by the guys outside, leant across and licked the inside of the window, ran his tongue over the length and breadth of a white dick that looked as thick and as long as Italy and, then in turn, a black one that had obviously put the horn into the horn of Africa.

Billy decided to simply turn off the engine. Like that, the car could go nowhere. He heard no one complaining, telling him to re-start his motor. It seemed to be the right signal. He heard both water-guns being turned off too. The drumming on the car's roof stopped although the guys remained as they were, grinding their dicks into the window glass on either side of Billy. Runnels of water dripped down the windshield, dropped off the rim of the roof. It was suddenly very quiet. Gingerly, Billy touched the buttons that operated the windows and both slid down a little. The noise of the electric motor was almost deafening.

This ploy seemed to excite both guys more. Billy hit the buttons again, enjoying the game, dropping the window a little at a time until the top of the glass had disappeared down into the door.

But which way to go first? Eeeny, meeny, miney ...mo!

Billy inclined his head and leant over, not very far, so that his mouth was an inch away from the white guy's dick. Billy could see easily beneath the thin fabric, saw unmistakably when the guy twitched his cock three or

Full Service

four times, like it was a signal, sort of making the eye in the head wink the obvious code for the signal, " ... and suck on this, fucker!"

Billy stuck out his tongue, flicked the tip of it lightly over the wet nylon. He sensed the guy outside bending in even closer, almost straining. But then what he couldn't see was that Janosh and Kukele were deep-tonguing each other over the top of the car's roof. All Billy noticed was Janosh's hand come down to flip down the elasticated coveralls and flip out a phallic feast fit for three.

Billy knelt on the carseat for an easier position and then fell onto Janosh's solid Czech dick, gobbling it down greedily, tonguing round the fold of heavy skin, pushing it back with little nips and kisses until the eastern Europe's best export potential was revealed, more valuable than all the grain in the Ukraine. Billy swallowed the cargo of Czech cock quicker than a freighter's hold as Janosh thrust deep in through the car window. The car started to rock. It was like being in an earthquake, Billy thought as he reached behind him, knowing full well that that way lay an equally venal feast. Kukele's cock was velvet, as long and thick as an equatorial night and it felt to Billy as though it was cut, foreskinless, its hard head coming to rest cleanly, like a heavy plum, into Billy's butterfly fingers.

Billy managed to force his mouth off Janosch's dick before pulling his sweats down around his ankles and then turning round, still kneeling on the driving seat and yet directing his appetite to the darker mountain of manhood which stood out like an ebony rolling-pin from Kukele's flat belly. Hungrily, Billy wasted no time, leaning forward and going straight down on the black wurst, pleased to hear a moan of pleasure from outside the car. He was also pleased to feel that his up-turned asshole hadn't gone unnoticed. He felt three fingers and then the fingers of another hand pulling the lips of his sphincter apart and probing, gently, into the glutinous pink tissue within.

Inside the office, Jimmy had lost no time. As soon as the door slid shut with that hiss of the hydraulic spring, Adam had very obviously rubbed his hand over the length of his dick as it lay, covered in CK boxer shorts along the length of his left thigh. Jimmy couldn't take his eyes off this unexpected and entirely welcome horizon. He started to play with himself too.

It was the start of rollercoaster, a ride that neither of them would be able to get off.

"Nice ...er, nice jeans," Jimmy said with a nervous, ingenuous grin, nodding his head downwards, to where Adam stood with his legs apart, raising himself up and down on his heels, making sure his hips were thrust out to best show-off his knob.

"Yeah. Bit tight, though. Whaddya think?"

"Oh, I... I, er ..." Jimmy stumbled over his words. He was salivating, licking his lips and swallowing all at the same time and uncontrollably, his legs started to shake and he dropped Adam's change he'd pulled out of the till. Three pound coins and a fifty pee rolled all over the wet, concrete floor. Jimmy dropped to his knees to retrieve the coins, thankful not to have to stand but amazed to find that Adam immediately moved closer to him so that there was no way Jimmy could not look at the blistering whiteness of the over-packed white denim crutch at his eyeline.

"Come on, get your mouth onto it," Adam growled, putting his hand firmly on top of Jimmy's tousled curls and forcing the young man's face to come to rest against the smooth cotton fabric. As he did so, with his right hand, he flipped the poppers on his fly. "Pull that fly back," he whispered to the kneeling Jimmy, "then get your tongue inside my shorts, yeah?" Adam pulled down his jeans so that they caught half-way down his thighs. His equally white CK boxers were cottony and freshly laundered with that smell of conditioner guys find so horny. Jimmy breathed deeply as his mouth opened wider and wider, taking the shaft of Adam's hugely engorged dick sideways on, like eating a hot dog the wrong way.

Adam peeled down the shorts by the waistband, stopping just at that point where Jimmy could see the start of the great cock, sunk like some giant tree's taproot into the dark hairy forest of the pubes which snaked down from his bellybutton.

"Lick the base of it first," Adam instructed as Jimmy expertly got his tongue inside the material of the shorts and started working the garment down, dragging a fold of it in his teeth, trying to tear through the last obstacle to suck-heaven.

"What about Billy?" Jimmy managed in all integrity to mumble. "I don'

Full Service

wanna butt in his act or anything ..."

"Jus' take a look outside," Adam suggested. "That should satisfy you." Adam could see over the top of where the tinting in the office glass ended. He could see what Billy was up to. Jimmy was kneeling just by the office door and he pulled it open.

"Oh ... right," he said and closed the door immediately. "In that case, put it in me mouth, then, yeah? I wanna get that down my throat like yesterday and keep it there for a week."

"Don't take too long," Adam urged, "'cos you're gonna get it rammed down your friggin' hole, too. I could fuck your cute little ass for a helluva lot longer than a week, believe me!"

And so Adam finally pulled out his knob, literally pulled it, like a hose being unwound from a garden reel and balanced the tip of it on the end of Jimmy's tongue, but not before Jimmy had gasped, felt his guts churn over. Jimmy tasted the huge dick, like it was the most fragile glass. Licked it like he would a strawberry drip-drop fresh with dew.

As Jimmy sank Adam's tool into his throat, Adam pulled off Jimmy's sweats and his hoody-top. He dragged the cotton vest roughly over the guy's nipples and then began to massage them, gently at first and then more precisely and firmly as he felt Jimmy squirm, felt that shudder of receptiveness vibrate through the young man's body, a spasm of eagerness which seemed to open Jimmy's throat even wider, allowing him to take even more of Adam's swollen prick into and down his vacuuming throat.

Adam looked over his shoulder to see through the office window that Billy, now naked but for his boots and his jockstrap, had gotten out of the car and was being led to the front of it by the black carwasher before being joined by the Czech. He watched as Billy was spread-eagled over the wet hood, saw his legs being spread apart. Jimmy's sucking time was almost through, Adam could feel it. He knew when a guy's throat had had enough of his all-but untakeable dick and he could feel Jimmy gagging, sensed a resistance each time he pushed Jimmy's head back down the length of his pole.

"You up for some real fun?" Adam suggested as Jimmy came up the last time for air.

"What d'you call this?" Jimmy grinned. "Best fun I've had since ... well, long story."

"Come with me," Adam said, pulling his jeans back up and taking the naked carwash boss's hand. They went outside, through the puddles of wet, dirty water and joined the other three at the car.

"Hi ...hi ...hi," Billy muttered, deep-down in his belly as the Czech man-rammer fucked at his hole, making the car sway backwards and forwards on its springs at each deep stab. "This what you call the full service, Jim?"

"Get down beside him," Adam commanded and bent Jimmy over double so that he joined Billy, the pair of them splayed out like some spatchcocked piece of schnitzel over the car.

"Did you get any lube?" Jimmy muttered, his sideways face almost matching Billy's as their cheeks felt the cold of the paintwork underneath them.

"I think he spat down my ass," Billy replied, handing over a rubber to Jimmy who reached back and felt the packet being taken out of his hand. But by who? Jimmy make it a rule never to shag the help. Never let the office pen be dipped in his own ink ... After a moment he felt someone's cock pressing at his asshole's outers.

"Can you see who it is, mate?" Jimmy mumbled. "Is it your mate?"

Billy, in a better position, looked up and saw Adam grinning, reaching forward to grip Jimmy's nipples.

"You're okay, Jim," Billy grinned and just as soon felt two huge arms grip him and pull him up so that he ended squatting against the Czech's flat hips, still pinned by the man's tireless dick. The black guy moved in front, grinned and said,

"Hi. I'm, Kukele. We haven't met."

"Pleasure's all mine, mate," Billy grinned as Kukele took Billy's legs, one in each hand and pressed them out, far enough so he could fit himself between Janosch and the car bumper. Billy felt a second force pressing at his humping gate and as he kissed Kukele hungrily, snogging him deeply, wetly with every inch of his tongue, he felt the big African enter him to lie alongside with Janosch. There wasn't much room to fuck but

Full Service

they all three twisted and squirmed and as far as Billy was concerned it was magic.

Adam was too busy to notice that Billy Stiles liked to be kissed. Far too busy.

"Oh, yeah!" Jimmy yelled. "Harder, please... Please! Pump me, fuck me, screw my ass! Oh!!!"

Adam was too excited to be polite for longer than he felt that he need be. He knew there would be other nights in this carwash, in that office. He heard the guys next to him moaning to the point of orgasm, knew Billy's tone when he was about to come. He pulled out of Jimmy's ass, turned him over just as Janosch and Kukele dropped Billy back on the hood and threw their rubbers to the ground, jerking themselves off the last few strokes home.

The three of them came in a splatter of white stuff over the two guys on the hood of the car, two guys who were kissing each other hungrily as they themselves shot dual fountains of spunk a moment or so later, geysering into the damp night air, layering the hood of the car with a finish to beat any carwash waxing in the world.

"Didn't know you was such a good kisser, Jimmy Chappell!" Billy exclaimed, panting, his face wreathed all about with a smile of deep satisfaction.

"You never asked me before," Jimmy replied.

TANTRIC SEX
by Dominic Santi

"Pick up coconut oil on your way home."

I almost creamed in my gym shorts. I turned quickly towards the wall behind the pay phone, trying to look nonchalant as I reached down between my legs and surreptitiously resituated myself, hoping not to draw too much attention to my sudden boner as I listened to the rest of my messages play back.

My lover, Jack, is into Tantric sex – that ancient Hindu stuff. He uses coconut oil when he strips me down and gives me one of his full body sexual massages. Just the thought of it makes my dick drip.

I'd never heard of Tantra before I met Jack. I'd just turned 22. I was working as a lifeguard, into the bar scene with my friends at night. Cruising was my life, and I didn't have any trouble finding other buff, young gym bunnies like myself.

So when this older guy – I guessed he was at least 30 – caught my eye one Friday night, I was surprised I paid any attention. Not my type, you know? But there was something about him. He looked good, for an older guy, and he was built.

I finally realised it was his eyes I couldn't look away from. They reminded me of the ocean after a storm – deep green, and hiding something very powerful roiling beneath a glass smooth surface. Those eyes were sparkling like the guy was looking at something he really enjoyed seeing. I realised that something was me.

I walked over and gave him my most winning smile. "You like?" I grinned.

"Very much," he said quietly. "Name's Jack." His voice was low and warm, and I liked his smile. I took his outstretched hand, mumbling "Cory" as I felt little tremors echo all the way to my nuts. It was weird. Not really lust,

Tantric Sex

yet more. I'd never felt anything like it.

I was still trying to figure it out when Jack slowly dragged his finger up my arm. His hand was hot, even through my shirt. My eyes widened as he turned his wrist and his finger brushed up the bare skin at the side of my neck.

"Shit!" I gasped, jumping so hard I almost spilled my drink. His touch felt like an electric shock.

Jack just laughed and moved his hand to the other side of my throat.

"How about you, Cory?" his eyes twinkled, though his voice was still quiet. "You like what you see?"

I nodded, once, unable to speak, but surprised that I meant it. I did like what I saw. He was about my height, short brown hair, handsome, in a rough outdoorsey sort of way. He wore a tight cotton sweater and jeans. Despite my usual attraction to guys my own age, I liked the way Jack's muscles looked. They weren't gym toned like mine, but they were fully developed – like he'd used them all his life until they'd matured into what they were supposed to be.

Jack's finger moved again, and he took the drink from my hand – a second before I would have dropped it. I grabbed his wrist to stop the shivers crawling back up my skin.

"How the hell do you do that?" I asked, trying to turn my head, but not quite making it. I couldn't believe how my body was reacting to him. Jack was playing with my earlobe, and each touch felt like he was tickling along the inside of my rapidly expanding dick.

"Your skin looks like it wants to be touched here," he laughed softly, stroking again as I shivered even harder. I glanced down. From the way Jack's jeans were bulging, I could tell he was getting turned on, too. He let his eyes travel slowly down me, then back up. My cock twitched like he'd licked it. I swear, I felt his eyes grazing over me even through my clothes. Then he leaned forward and gently took my earlobe between his lips, sucking softly.

"I can show your body lots of places it would like to be touched." His tongue darted inside my ear, hitting some nerve that almost made me come. I gasped and closed my eyes, shuddering so hard my teeth shook.

"Come back to my place with me, Cory. I'll touch every inch of your skin, just like this." Jack's fingernail scratched a spot I didn't know existed behind my ear. I moaned as I felt an ooze of pre-cum leak out of my dick.

"I promise you, it'll take at least three hours and I'll bring you to the brink of orgasm six times before I let you come."

"Oh, Christ," I choked, leaning into his touch. His finger kept moving, scratching lightly, making my skin crawl towards him, pulling me towards him, until I gasped out, "Yes."

I said it again and again, until it was like part of my breathing. I don't know how long we stood there at the corner of the bar. We weren't even kissing, he was just making love to my ears. Eventually, one of my friends came over to check on me. We watch out for each other, you know? As I came up for air, Jack quietly tucked a business card in my buddy's pocket and said, "My home number is on the back. Call him tomorrow if you want."

I vaguely remember wondering why the hell Jack figured I'd still be at his place in the morning. He put his arm around my shoulder, letting his thumb skim lightly over my shirt, just brushing the nipple. I shuddered, trying to keep my eyes focused. Somewhere in the back of my mind, I heard him say, "I'll take good care of him." By then, I was in such a lust-induced trance all I could do was nod to my friends. I was ready to follow Jack anywhere.

His apartment was like something out of a martial arts movie. A single lamp glowed on the wall, casting just enough light for me to see the large open futon, covered with black satin sheets, that doubled as a couch in the centre of the main room. I liked the idea of somebody who set up his living space around his bed.

Jack had kicked off his sandals as he'd walked in the door. I followed suit, leaning against the wall and unlacing my boots as Jack moved quietly around the room. Pretty soon, sandalwood incense tickled my nostrils. I love that smell, it always reminds me of fucking on the beach. By the time I stepped into the middle of the room, soft flute music was playing in the background.

Jack paused in lighting some candles to smile over his shoulder at me. "You'll enjoy this more if you're cleaned out. The bathroom's down the hall if you need to take care of anything."

"After the fact," I blushed, glad I'd even stopped to pee as we left the bar. "I planned on partying tonight."

Tantric Sex

"You'll like this better than a party," he laughed. Jack flicked off the light, then he turned to me and slid his hands slowly up my arms.

"Trust me, Cory. You'll like this a lot."

As soon as he touched me, I was shivering again. He ran his fingers along the base of my hair, until he came to that spot he'd found in back of my ear. I closed my eyes as his voice crawled over my skin.

"Tonight, I want you to be selfish, Cory. I want you to give in to your senses completely – just relax and feel. Can you do that for me?"

"Uh, huh," I nodded, my cock so hard again that it was bending almost painfully down my leg. With what Jack was doing to my ears, I would have walked across a bed of burning coals for him, even though he wasn't making a lot of sense. I mean, I can be as self-centred as the next guy in bed, but I'd never consciously set out to ignore my partner before.

"What about you?" I whispered, wiggling under his fingers.

"Don't you get off on this?"

I heard the smile in his voice.

"My pleasure will come from watching you."

Well, when he put it that way, it seemed fair enough. Besides, I figured I could massage him later if that's what he wanted. I've been told I give a mean backrub.

I moaned as his other hand skimmed across my pec towards my nipple. At that point, I'd have done damn near anything for him.

Damn near. I grabbed his wrist.

"Latex," I gasped, figuring that was the one thought I had to hold onto, no matter how much I was thinking with my dick.

"Of course," he laughed. "I doubt you'll notice it. But open your eyes and double check any time you want."

"Okay," I said lamely. My brain was total mush.

Jack laughed, tickling my neck until my dick oozed again.

"Three hours, and six times to the brink before you come," he whispered. "Relax."

Then he touched his soft, wet lips to mine. He kissed me until I could hardly breathe.

I'm not really sure how we got undressed. I was shivering from his touch, shivering more as my clothes fell away and I felt his hands on my naked skin. The next thing I knew, I was lying on the cool satin sheets, and Jack was kneeling beside the futon, squeezing oil onto his hands. It smelled like suntan lotion. I opened my eyes as my nose wrinkled.

"Coconut oil. It's good for your skin," he said, setting the bottle down on the bed. "You have a beautiful body."

"Thanks. I work out a lot." Hours and hours each week, but I didn't say that. I was glad he appreciated the time I put into looking so good. He looked pretty fine naked, too. His body was smooth, with stiff brown nips glowing in the candlelight. I could see where he'd brushed them with oil. I started to reach for them. They mesmerised me, like magnets. But he shook his head, and I let my hands fall back on the sheets. I watched his fingers move towards my left pec, jumped nervously when he touched me. Then I relaxed into the warmth of his palm.

"With a body like this, you should take better care of yourself."

My eyes flew up as he stroked firmly down over my abdomen, circling three times before he moved back up to my chest. "Too much red meat, too much alcohol. They make you too tense. A body like this deserves better care."

Talk about interrupting the mood!

"Well, if you don't like it," I sputtered, getting up onto my elbows.

"I didn't say that," he laughed.

I would have laid back down anyway, even if it weren't for the light pressure of his hand on my chest. Well, I would have. Probably. I blushed as my head touched the pillow again. Jack's eyebrow flickered approvingly at the erection poking up proudly towards my belly.

"I just said you should take better care of yourself. Shhhh." The trace of his frown locked my protest inside my lips. He was stroking my chest and abs again. One hand travelled lightly between my legs, brushing the top of my erection and coming to rest cupping my scrotum.

"Perfect pecs, tight abs, way more than a handful down here. A body like this should be cared for and appreciated for a long time." He blew softly towards his hand, letting his breath tickle across my balls. "Let me show you a long time."

Tantric Sex

His hands started massaging me, and I didn't have the strength to talk anymore. Jack turned my whole body into warm, sweet butter. He massaged my eyebrows and my cheekbones, kneaded the oil deep into my scalp until my skin felt like it was reaching towards him. The music had changed to something that sounded like the ocean ebbing and flowing on a quiet night. I love the sound of the water. Pretty soon, it was hard to keep my eyes open. I quit trying and let them close.

"Breathe with me," he said. I did, following his directions – using my strength for the inhale and then letting the air flow back out of me on its own – until I felt like I was floating. After that, Jack didn't say anything for a long time. He worked his way down my torso. His hands talked to me, telling me how much he enjoyed my body. It felt so good that at first I didn't realise I'd gone completely soft.

Until Jack said, "This next part will work best if you don't let yourself get all the way hard. Lie back and enjoy."

I looked down, and sure enough, my "seven inches when it's stiff" dick was cuddled up against my balls like a fat caterpillar taking a nap. Jack lifted it between his thumb and forefinger, pressing it firmly between them.

"This will wake you up," he said.

It sure did. The blood rushed into my dick. Then he started massaging my shaft like it was the hand on a clock. Midnight. He pointed me upwards and stroked the underside of my shaft. Long, full brushes all up the length of his palm. Damn, it felt good. Two. Three. He turned my dick towards the side and stroked the surface facing his hand. I was getting hard again, fast. By six, I was moaning, bent downwards, harder than was "optimal," my slit pointing towards my toes. When he was done massaging the top of my shaft, he wrapped his hand around me and milked me like a cow's teat.

I groaned. I was almost too hard to bend that way. But Jack didn't stop. And he didn't do any stroke long enough to make me come. Pretty soon I shivered just at the sound of the oil bottle squeezing. The air would fill with a puff of coconut smell, then I'd feel the warm oil sliding off his newly slicked hands as he changed strokes.

When he pulled my skin taut, holding it at the base of my shaft, then jacking me lightly with his other hand, I almost came on the spot. I gasped, arching up as I felt my nuts starting to churn.

"Not yet," Jack said firmly, squeezing hard, right at the base of my cock.

I groaned again, my body protesting loudly as it crawled back from the edge. I opened my eyes to see Jack laughing softly at me.

"We're nowhere near three hours yet." He leaned over and licked the inside of my thigh. "This is just a taste."

The sound I made, somewhere between a moan and a cry, just made him laugh. Then his hands were all over my thighs, and my belly, and my chest. When I got my breathing back under control, he reached between my legs again. One o'clock. Six. Eleven. He rubbed the palm of his hand across the cap of my glans, smearing the pre-cum leaking from my piss slit into the coconut oil he was kneading into my skin. He played my nipples and nuts, tickling and teasing and pinching, until my dick jumped and oozed pre-cum at the lightest feather touch of his fingertips. He woke up parts of my genitals I didn't know I had. And believe me, I thought I'd explored every possible inch of that area. I was wrong.

My muscles were quivering like Jell-O when Jack rolled me over onto my side. He lifted my top leg up, bending it over until my knee rested on the bed. I groaned so loudly I would have been really embarrassed if I hadn't been so completely relaxed. Except for my cock, which was rebelliously ignoring Jack's "don't get too hard" directions. I moaned even louder as the side of his hand slid down the crack of my ass.

"Now for the anal massage, Cory."

This time, the sound I made was loud, and it was all pure pleasure. Jack's hand glided back and forth. I heard the smile in his voice, but I didn't have the energy to do anything but gasp and leak more pre-cum. His fingers were magic. They played with my asslips like tongues, kissing every little flutter. I couldn't figure out what I liked best – the little circles with his fingertips, or the long, slow stretches where the fingers of his right hand pulled one way and the fingers of his left pulled the other way. I guess my body talked to him, though, because no matter what other strokes he did, Jack always kept coming back to those two. Pretty soon, my asshole was so hungry for his touch that I was moaning almost constantly.

"Do you want more, Cory?" His voice slid over my skin. "Do you want my fingers in you?"

"Please," I whispered. It was hard to make my mouth form the words. I groaned as another hot ooze of pre-cum slid out of my dick.

"Do you want me to massage your pleasure centre – your joyspot? It will feel very good when I touch you inside."

"Oh, God, yes." His voice made me shiver, like a tambourine that's been struck. My asshole was so damn hungry. I jumped at the sound of a glove being snapped on. Smelled the puff of the coconut oil.

"Ahhhh!" my cry almost drowned out Jack's laughter as his finger slid into me. His touch was pure sensation. I almost came. I think maybe I did, just a little, just my asshole, if that's even possible. It shivered and spasmed like a mini climax as he slid into me. Man, his fingers knew their way around. Within minutes, it felt like they'd spent eons learning how to tease every nerve that came anywhere near my rectum into quivering insanity. His fingers were firm and strong. They knew just where to press and push and stroke, and caress. He brought me to the brink once, twice. I was shocked to hear my own voice chanting, "fuck me, fuck me," like some sort of obscene porn-vid mantra.

Jack kept three fingers buried to the hilt in me as he flipped me over on my back.

"Lift your knees, up and back," he commanded.

I knew the moves like I knew my name, but I was surprised at how hard it was to make my hands obey me. My skin was lost in the sensations emanating from my asshole.

"I want to come," I pleaded.

"That's only three."

I could hear the lust in Jack's voice as he spoke. I forced my eyes open to see him kneeling between my legs, his erection pointing straight out and a strand of pre-cum drooling off the tip onto the bed. He was gorgeous. He was so fucking hot. My whole body lurched just looking at him. Thank God Jack's fingers were only resting inside of me. I swear, that was the only reason he was able to grab me and squeeze the climax from spurting out of me.

My cry of frustration was broken only by his laughter. "Four."

Then he was back to doing that damned clock massage again. This time, my dick knew what to expect. It was almost impossible to stay flexible enough for positions five through seven. His finger curled over my joyspot just as he milked position six downward. The direction saved me, that and Jack's hand clamping tight again. I almost couldn't pull back. My prostate was screaming. It wanted to come. I needed to come. NOW!

"Please!" I begged. "Please, please, PLEASE!" I was almost screaming, I needed it so bad. The biggest come of my life was building up in my balls. I gripped my knees to my shoulders, hugging them hard like I could maybe press the climax out that way if Jack wouldn't give me that one extra little touch that my body needed to explode.

Then Jack's hands were moving again. He'd slathered them with oil. He had four fingers in me. I was stretched so wide my asshole was gaping. His thumb rested on my perineum, massaging my prostate from the outside while his fingers did the same from the inside. His other hand, slick with oil, was wrapped around my dick, stroking again. Pulling the climax right up out of my spine.

"Once more to the edge, Cory. Then you can come."

I groaned so loudly I almost cried. Not just to the edge. Not again. I couldn't stand it again! The pressure was building. He pressed my joyspot. My juices oozed. My dick strained into his hand. He stroked. Hot. I was boiling inside.

"To the edge..."

I screamed. I couldn't stand it. I needed to come – needed, needed, NEEDED!

"Over!" he snapped.

My body erupted. The juice boiled up out of my prostate and I came, yelling at the top of my lungs, as Jack pulled the best orgasm of my life through every shrieking, quivering nerve in my cock. Every last drop of semen in my body emptied itself into Jack's waiting hand. My body shook so hard I thought my bones would break, and I kept shaking, even after my cock was empty.

When I could finally breathe again, I opened my eyes, letting my legs collapse back down onto the bed. Jack was smiling at me, his body hunched forward, large glops of his own come dripping down off of his nipples. Talk about a turn on. Man, the guy came just from watching me shoot!

Tantric Sex

A glance at the clock told me we really had been at it for three fucking hours. It barely registered. All I wanted to do was sleep. I curled up into his arms, so drained I didn't think I'd be able to get hard for a week.

We waited until the next morning to do it again. When my friends called around noon, I was still there, watching a video on how to do the massages on Jack. Then I started practicing on him. And he practiced more on me.

That was three years ago. I'm still here. My name is on the apartment lease now. I've been a vegetarian for a long time, and I don't drink much anymore. But I still work out at the gym every day.

And I'm definitely picking up coconut oil on my way home tonight.

ABOUT THE AUTHORS

Alex Corey has written for ADVOCATE CLASSIFIEDS and various anthologies, including ROUGH AND READY. He lives in New York City.

Jameson Currier is the author of the novel WHERE THE RAINBOW ENDS (Overlook) and the story collection DANCING ON THE MOON (Viking). His short stories have appeared in many anthologies, including THE MAMMOTH BOOK OF GAY EROTICA, STOCKING STUFFERS, FEELING FRISKY, ROUGH AND READY, MEN ON MEN 5, BEST GAY EROTICA 1996, 1997, and 1998, THE MAN OF MY DREAMS, and others. He regularly contributes essays, articles, and reviews to many periodicals across the country, and is currently working as an associate editor for the NEW YORK BLADE.

David Evans is author of the novels SUMMER SET (Millivres), A CAT IN THE TULIPS (Millivres), and the forthcoming THE OTHER SIDE OF SUNSET. He is also the author of biographies of Dusty Springfield, Cat Stevens, and Freddie Mercury, and writing under the pseudonym Ned Creswell, the novel A HOLLYWOOD CONSCIENCE. He lives in London, England.

Michael Lassell is the award-winning author of a collection of (mostly erotic) stories, CERTAIN ECSTASIES (Painted Leaf Press); three collections of poetry, A FLAME FOR THE TOUCH THAT MATTERS (Painted Leaf), DECADE DANCE, and POEMS FOR LOST AND UN-LOST BOYS; and a collection of essays, stories, and poems, THE HARD WAY (Richard Kasak Books). He is also the editor of the anthologies MEN SEEKING MEN: ADVENTURES IN GAY PERSONALS (Painted Leaf) and, with Lawrence Schimel, TWO HEARTS DESIRE: GAY COUPLES ON THEIR LOVE (St. Martin's Press), as well as two gay poetry anthologies, THE NAME OF LOVE (St. Martin's Press) and EROS IN BOYSTOWN (Crown). His writing has appeared in many anthologies, including AROUSED, ROUGH AND READY, THE MAMMOTH BOOK OF GAY EROTICA, THE BADBOY BOOK OF EROTIC POETRY, MEN ON MEN 3, and both the BEST GAY EROTICA andFLESH AND THE WORD series, as well as in numerous periodicals. He lives in New York City, where he works as an editor for METROPOLITAN HOMES magazine.

Chris Leslie is the publisher of DIRTY magazine, which can be found on the web at http://www.banjee.com/ His work has also appeared in various periodicals and anthologies, including THE MAMMOTH BOOK OF GAY EROTICA, STALLIONS AND OTHER STUDS, S/X, and THE EVERARD REVIEW, among others. He makes a living as a graphic designer in New York City.

Dominic Santi is a Los Angeles-based freelance writer whose stories have appeared in numerous anthologies–including HARD AT WORK, THE YOUNG AND THE HUNG, SEX TOY TALES, THE EROTIC WEB: THREADS FROM THE INTERNET, and THE MAMMOTH BOOK OF HISTORICAL EROTICA–as well as in various magazines, including ADVOCATE MEN, IN TOUCH, FIRSTHAND, and PENTHOUSE VARIATIONS. Santi is also section leader for Alternative Eros in CompuServe's Erotica forum.

Lawrence Schimel is an award-winning author and anthologist whose books include THE MAMMOTH BOOK OF GAY EROTICA (Robinson), THE DRAG QUEEN OF ELFLAND (Circlet Press), SWITCH HITTERS: LESBIANS WRITE GAY MALE EROTICA AND GAY MEN WRITE LESBIAN EROTICA (with Carol Queen; Cleis Press), PoMoSEXUALS: CHALLENGING ASSUMPTIONS ABOUT GENDER AND SEXUALITY (with Carol Queen; Cleis Press), and TWO HEARTS DESIRE: GAY COUPLES ON THEIR LOVE (with Michael Lassell; St. Martin's Press), among others. His work is included in more than 160 anthologies, such as BEST GAY EROTICA 97 and 98, THE RANDOM HOUSE BOOK OF SCIENCE FICTION STORIES, THE RANDOM HOUSE TREASURY OF LIGHT VERSE, GAY LOVE POETRY, SHAKESPEAREAN DETECTIVES, and THE MAMMOTH BOOK OF FAIRY TALES, among many others. Occasionally, he also writes for periodicals, and he has contributed to publications as diverse as THE SATURDAY EVENING POST, PHYSICS TODAY, and DRUMMER. He lives in Madrid.

Don Shewey has published three books, including OUT FRONT, the Grove Press anthology of gay and lesbian plays. His erotic stories have appeared in the anthologies THE MAMMOTH BOOK OF GAY EROTICA, HARD AT WORK, ROUGH AND READY, THE YOUNG AND THE HUNG, and FLASHPOINT, among others. He has written extensively for the VILLAGE VOICE and THE ADVOCATE and has taught theatre at New York University. He lives in New York City, where in addition to writing he makes a living as a professional bodyworker.

ABOUT THE EDITOR

David Laurents is the editor of the anthologies HARD AT WORK, ROUGH AND READY, FEELING FRISKY, THE YOUNG AND THE HUNG, THE BAD-BOY BOOK OF EROTIC POETRY, WANDERLUST: HOMOEROTIC TALES OF TRAVEL, and SOUTHERN COMFORT. His erotic short stories and poems have been published in many magazines, including Drummer, Torso, Mandate, First Hand, and Gay Scotland, as well as in various anthologies, including FLASHPOINT, SPORTSMEN, MY THREE BOYS, MAD ABOUT THE BOYS, PLAY HARD, and others. He lives in New York City.

ACKNOWLEDGMENTS

"Vector Experiments" © 1998 Alex Corey. First published in ADVOCATE MEN. Reprinted by permission of the author.

"Lessons" © 1999 by Jameson Currier. First published, in an earlier version, in MEN SEEKING MEN, edited by Michael Lassell. Reprinted by permission of the author.

"Practice Pony" © 1995 by Lawrence Schimel. First published in MANDATE. Reprinted by permission of the author.

"Snowbound" © 1999 by Dominic Santi. Reprinted by permission of the author.

"Mind Over Matter" © 1997 by Chris Leslie. First published in DIRTY. Reprinted by permission of the author.

"In the Pitts" © 1998 by Michael Lassell. Reprinted by permission of the author.

"Daddy Lover God" © 1999 by Don Shewey. Reprinted by permission of the author.

"Full Service" © 1997 by David Evans. Reprinted by permission of the author.

"Tantric Sex" © 1998 by Dominic Santi. First published in ADVOCATE MEN. Reprinted by permission of the author.